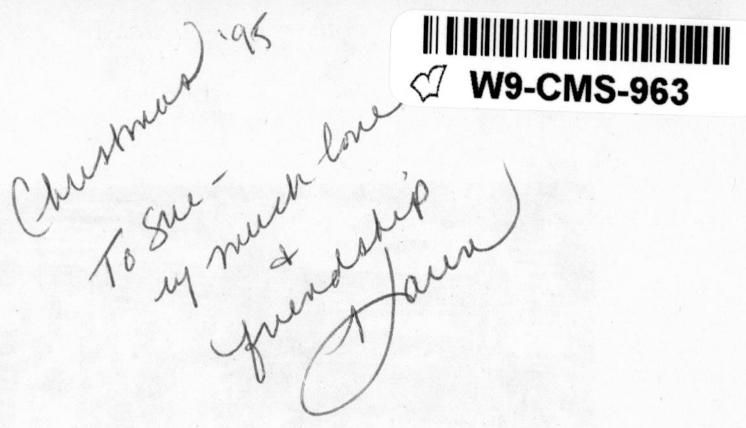

The I of the Beholder

Stephen Vicchio

As an individual, each of us is a fragment of a species, a part of the universe, a unique point in the immense web of the cosmic, ethical, and historical forces and influences, and we are bound by their laws. Although what makes us individuals derives from matter, what makes us persons derives from the realm of the spirit.

Jacques Maritain

The I of the Beholder

Essays and Stories

Stephen Vicchio

Cathedral Foundation Press
Baltimore

Printed and bound in the United States of America

1 2 3 4 5 04 03 02 01 00 99 98 97 96 95

Library of Congress Cataloging-in-Publication Data

Vicchio, Stephen.
The I of the beholder : essays and stories / Stephen Vicchio.
p. cm.
ISBN 1-885938-24-1 (pbk.)
I. Title
AC8.V415 1995 95-36918
081--dc20 CIP

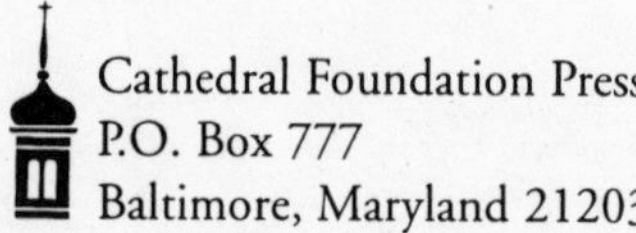
Cathedral Foundation Press
P.O. Box 777
Baltimore, Maryland 21203

Book design by Sue Seiler
Cover design by Steve Fabijanski
Backcover photograph by Denise Walker

Other Books by Stephen Vicchio

**Ordinary Mysteries* (Westminster, Md.: Wakefield Editions, 1991)

The Voice from the Whirlwind: The Problem of Evil in the Modern World (Westminster, Md.: Christian Classics, 1989)

**Perspectives on the American Catholic Church 1789-1989*, co-edited with Sr. Virgina Geiger (Westminster, Md.: Christian Classics, 1989)

A Careful Disorder: Chronicles of Life, Love and Laughter (Westminster, Md.: Christian Classics, 1987)

Noted (*) titles are available from Catholic Books, etc. For more information, call (410) 547-5324.

Contents

Foreword

"I am alive!" wrote a Norwegian prisoner in a German concentration camp, in a large hand, filling the one piece of paper he was allowed for a letter. In her autobiography of resistance, *Walls*, Hiltgunt Zassenhaus tells of meeting this prisoner, months after she had censured him. He told her it was written on the day he was condemned to death. But at that writing he was alive! And his defiant spirit, unfettered in his incarceration, leapt from the page.

It is in the realm of the spirit that we truly live and move and have our being.

In essays marked by simplicity of style and complexity of thought, Stephen Vicchio shares with the reader incidents in his life, and the reflections which they engender. By revealing himself, he makes the reader conscious of what "the realm of the spirit" really means, and how this realm identifies a person as clearly as a thumbprint. And yet, as thumbs are common to everyone, so these essays and stories—at once personal and universal—illuminate our common humanity.

For we are all "beholders," and although the eye, the organ of sight, is the human feature that unites us, the "I" of the spirit is the great individuator. The gift of any essayist, and the unique charm of Stephen Vicchio, lies in the communication of an individual yet universal view of reality .

Flannery O'Connor, a story-teller of great distinction, wrote with deep perception about the human eye. She said it had roots in the soul, and she used her considerable power of description to reveal a character's soul by delineating his eyes. In the last story she wrote before her death, "Parker's

Back," she sketched the souls of a God-hungry vagrant, O.E. Parker, and his fundamentalist wife with telling description. Parker's eyes "were the same pale slate-color as the ocean, and reflected the immense spaces around him as if they were a microcosm of the mysterious sea." Sarah Ruth's eyes "were gray and sharp like the points of two ice picks." One was open to the mystery of God's action in his life; the other had all the answers. The description of their eyes foreshadows the story's tragic, yet redemptive, conclusion.

O'Connor sums up her own talent, and, by extension, Stephen Vicchio's talent, when she writes, "Everything has its testing point in the eye, an organ which eventually involves the whole personality and as much of the world as can be got into it." In *The I of the Beholder,* the reader looks through the eyes and the soul of a lover of the world and its people, and sees a new vision of reality. The everyday world takes on a patina produced by Stephen Vicchio's spirit. His vision is sometimes wry, sometimes tender, often humorous, and always faith-filled.

These essays and stories should be read as most of them were published: as single, stand-alone pieces. The impact is stronger if they are read singly, followed by the reader's own reflections. For in drawing from literature, history, philosophy, popular culture, nature, family life, politics, science, and religion, Stephen Vicchio opens up vast fields of our own thinking, and the feelings that our thoughts will generate. We impoverish ourselves if we do not mine the ore revealed by the thrusts of his diamond-sharp intellect.

There are many ways of teaching. Stephen Vicchio

extends his remarkable teaching career in these essays. From reading them and mulling them over, I have learned to see more clearly what my eyes behold, and to make the connections which distinguish me as a person. To every reader this gift is offered.

Sr. Kathleen Feeley, SSND

former President
College of Notre Dame of Maryland

Executive Director
The Caroline Center
Baltimore

Preface

The I of the Beholder

He who loves the beautiful is called a lover because he partakes in that which inspires him.

Plato
Phaedrus

A work of art is good if it has sprung from necessity. In this nature of its origin lies in its judgment. There is no other.

Rainer Maria Rilke
Letters to a Young Poet

I was introduced to the intricacies of English grammar and composition by nuns with names like Perfecta and Redemptina. In religion class these sturdy women might have been fully aware of the Augustinian principle that we are all fallen and imperfect creatures, but that did not stop them from exhibiting a more Pelagian attitude when it came to the finer points of grammar and syntax. "Salvation by works" was the rule of the day in English class, and it was only to be gained with the use of the active voice, and through a strict avoidance of the practice of joining independent clauses with unsightly commas.

Long before I knew about Strunk and White, and a few

years before Warrener's *English Grammar* made pimples only my second biggest problem in high school, the good nuns were writing helpful suggestions all over my black and white marble grade school theme books. The margins of a copy book, like the grill-work opening of a confessional box, is no place to mince words, so the sisters gave it to me straight in unmistakable and perfectly slanted Palmer method: avoid needless words; make sure you have a beginning, middle, and end; do not end a sentence with a preposition; and only write about the things you know.

I published my first essay over two decades ago. Since that time, I have been trying to follow the nuns' advice. I have never managed to fully appreciate, however, one of their rules for successful writing: thou shalt never use the first person, singular pronoun. Just spend a moment glancing again over this introduction; already I have broken this commandment ten times and I am only in the third paragraph.

The good sisters were not alone in their disdain for the use of the personal pronoun. Even in his most lyrical and personal essays, E.B. White obediently follows the rule, but I have not been able to manage it. Me, myself, and I are all over the essays I have produced in the past twenty-five years. I do not know how to write in the third person, any more than I know how to breathe out of another's lungs; nor can I think of myself, despite living in an age of supposed rampant multiple personality disorders, as a plural.

The editorial "we" always has seemed to me a curious and unsuccessful place to hide, like the use of the passive voice, or like a five-year-old who plays hide-and-seek by immediately returning to the same closet at the start of every game. I have often wondered whether the Queen of England really does speak in the royal "we." Does she actually say things like, "You know, we really must have our throne dry-cleaned before the Christmas holidays," or "Philip, our grace, could you pass us the scones?"

In a real way, my discomfort with the use of the editorial "we" is the genesis of the title of this book. I have named it *The I of the Beholder* because I wish it to convey something of the personal character of these essays. In the best of personal essays, you find no disclaimers as you often do in other kinds of writing. The personal pronouns are the stuff of which the essay is made. The essayist would never think of saying anything like "This is only my personal opinion," for what else is there?

It is, of course, "beauty" that is to be found in the eye of the beholder. In many of the pieces here I have wrestled as best I can with ways of showing the things in my life that I find uncommonly beautiful, true, and good. Since the publication in 1991 of my last book of essays, *Ordinary Mysteries*, my family has grown to include a second son, Reed Cahill Vicchio. Much of what I find beautiful these days is bound up with my family and their extraordinary capacity to amaze and delight me, and to make me laugh, even at myself.

I have written the essays found here over the last four years. In that time, our country has fought and won a war in the Persian Gulf, we have changed presidents, the economy has rebounded, and the World Series was canceled for the first time in modern baseball history. These events, and many others, have provided me with ample opportunity to practice the good sisters' rules for good writing.

Among other things, you will find her my ruminations about Holocaust denial and the roots of evil, and why Mickey Mouse wears trousers, while Donald Duck does not. You will also find reminiscences about dressing as a devil for my third grade Halloween party, some reflections about my wife's apparent addiction to the five-day weather forecast, an essay on the relationship between love and certain kinds of memory, and a short piece on the comforts and blessings of silence.

Above all, what I hope you find here is a teacher and writer, a husband and father who cares deeply about many things, but mostly about his family, about the craft of writing, and about the alchemical practice of good teaching. Walter Bagehot in his *Literary Studies* suggests that a teacher "should have an atmosphere of awe, and walk wonderingly, as if he was amazed at being himself." Most times, I think of my life as so filled with grace and the goodness of others—my students, my family, my friends—that I am almost always amazed at being myself.

Many of these essays and stories first appeared in other places. I am grateful to the *Baltimore Sun* and *Sun Magazine*, the *Evening Sun*, *America*, *Today*, *Catholic Digest*, *Style*, *The Critic*, *The Quill*, and *Baltimore* magazine for their permission to reprint them here.

This book came about at the suggestion of Andrew Ciofalo and Gregg Wilhelm. I am grateful to them for their advice and friendship. Jessica Crimmins, Anysia Marcell, Kim Quantmeyer, and Rebecca Roberson worked many hours in preparing the manuscript. In addition to providing me with my first full-time employment, I am also indebted to Sr. Kathleen Feeley for the kind remarks she has provided in the foreword. Toni Adashi introduced me to the work of Frans Mazereel, a twentieth-century Belgian artist. I have included a number of his most evocative woodcuts in the beginning of each of the chapters.

My wife, Kathleen Cahill, and our two boys, Owen and Reed, continue to make me a vessel into which they pour so much of their goodness. Chesterton was correct when he called family "the first and only real source of preservation and healing."

Finally, I wish to thank three women: Sister Bridget Marie, Sister Maura, and Sister Virgina, my colleagues at the College of Notre Dame of Maryland. I have watched their goodness and beauty for many years. Coming to know them, all they stand for, and all they are, has been as important for me as truth itself. It is to these three scholars this book is dedicated.

Baltimore
Fourth of July
1995

Chapter

One

On the Sea

Thou glorious mirror, where the Almighty's form glasses itself in tempests: in all time, calm and convulsed—in breeze or gale, or storm, icing the pole, or in the torrid clime dark-heaving—boundless, endless, and sublime.

George Byron

This book begins at sea in much the same way that each of our lives does. Most of the world's ancient mythologies bring our origins back to Mother Oceanus. My family, too, returns each summer to the sea. It is a time when my marriage, my vocation as a teacher, and my life as a father are all annually re-baptized. The pieces collected in this first chapter tell something of those sacred times spent with Mother Oceanus.

Returning to the Sea

If there is magic to be found on this planet, it is contained in water.

Loren Eiseley
The Immense Journey

By the time the screen door swings back to make its thud, already I have bounded down the wooden steps. A moment later, on the path leading over the dune line, I pass stubborn tufts of saw grass hedged in by battered snow fences.

I cover the hundred yards of sand between dune line and ocean like a weary man finishing a desert crossing. Then, an awkward dive, the shock of cold water, a few strokes to move me beyond the breakers, and I am overtaken, consumed, returned to the sea.

Immediately I hear the ocean's surfy, slow, deep mellow voice. It is full of mystery and awe, mourning over the dead it holds in its bosom. Yet it promises new life. I float along on my back for several minutes, my mind emptied of everything but water. In Egyptian hieroglyphics the symbol for water is a wavy line with small, sharp crests. Three wavy lines stand for the primeval mother ocean, Nu, from which we all have come.

In the cosmology of the ancient Mesopotamians the great sea was regarded as a symbol of the unfathomable. The name for the ancient Celtic god Domnu meant "deep water." The writers of the biblical book of Job believed the answers to the mystery of human suffering and the meaning of life were to be found at the bottom of the ocean. In the Hindu sacred writings, the *Vedas,* water is referred to as Matritachmah, "the most maternal," for in the beginning everything was like a sea without light.

In a few moments my mind turns to another ocean, or perhaps it is the same one, growing inside my wife. Hers is a salt sea in which there floats a tiny voyager. We know the small swimmer is a boy. Ultrasound has opened a window to the womb. And with it has come new exhilaration and new worry. The proportion of salt in the boy's amniotic ocean is precisely the same as in the greater sea to which I have come to lose myself, and the worry, for a while.

I float along thinking about the world into which he will come, about the love he must already feel, about how that love alone will not be enough to make him safe. I float along wondering if he will love the sea as much as I do.

From the smaller sea and the greater sea we all have come. Five hundred years before Christ, the Greek philosopher Anaximander, a man who lived by the sea, suggested we all began as fish. Among the ancient Babylonians, Oannes, the mythical creature who brought culture to human-kind, was portrayed as half man and half fish.

The pregnancy picture books and Darwin's *Descent of Man* tell the same tale: ontogeny recapitulates phylogeny—each individual in its development tells the story of the entire race. Nature has sent us forth from the watery womb into a region of light, like sailors miraculously cast ashore from a dark and mysterious mother sea.

Before the boy existed, before he began to float inside my wife, trading his nothingness for the possibility of everything, there was only an egg smaller than the period at the end of this sentence. Then millions of tiny swimmers, like persistent salmon, searched for that single grain of ovarian sand. A solitary swimmer, with the tail flashing, found the shore. Now the boy floats inside my wife.

The boy floats along and I float along thinking of the boy floating along. We are both waiting for new life. I begin to understand, as if for the first time, that the very commonplaces of life are precisely what constitutes its greatest mystery. That there is something rather than nothing is perhaps the greatest mystery of all.

In the Beginning

For a web begun God sends thread.

Italian proverb

It started in the spring, though his beginning, like the world's, was necessarily tangled and chaotic—tiny swimmers searching in a briny sea, their tails waging in a microscopic quest for life. One persistent swimmer found mother-land, and my wife had company inside her skin. Nothing ever begins when we think it did.

In the Middle Ages, cloistered monks debated whether it was possible for God to create something out of nothing. My wife and I created a unicellular something, made from nothing but passion and the hand of the Divine.

By the summer, he had grown to a tadpole of a boy, swimming inside his mother. At our retreat by the shore, my wife also floated on a great sea. Her red hair salty wet, she bobbed above, then below the crest. In the air, the gulls hung suspended—wings frozen against the wind. She floated on the sea, a shining jewel, an unknown child in her flesh. She floated and dreamed, a mother ocean.

In the fall, life swelled downward. She became a vase, filled with salt water and one small bud. She stood as winter wheat bending down toward the earth. She lay on her side, a mare with tiny hooves beating against her ribs, until, in the dead of winter, he burst forth.

If the boy had entered the world with the gifts of memory and speech, he might have told fantastic tales, as strange as those of Ulysses washed up on his mother shore. But the tiny boy held his tongue. A silence hung in the air, like the interval between crashing waves. His half-opened eyes screamed, "Don't touch me," yet at the same time they implored, "Don't leave me." Washed up on the strange coast, he thought he had better be careful about getting to know the natives.

The mundane quickly followed the miraculous. The joy of seeing his toothless grin, or of first finding the downy fuzz on the nape of his neck, was overtaken by the first cold, by teething, and by dead-of-night feedings as regular and unforgiving as the mortgage payment. Time for examining the swirl of a tiny fingerprint gave way to routine needle-prickings at the doctor's office. First came the miracle, then the realization that even miracles suffer everyday insults.

His life unfolds too quickly. It is a broken spigot gushing at full force. Days turn quietly into months, and I feel the mystery slipping away. His life came miraculously rising, a creature bathed in light, out of the dark sea, utterly new and fresh and astounding. And then he was sent a social security number. He was clothed in plastic diapers. His appointments were written on a small calendar on the refrigerator.

Five months later we need to recover the miraculous, so we return to the sea. Steel gray clouds mingle like spirits that, in the beginning, moved across the face of the water. At water's edge, a gentle salt breeze turns from the north and the tiny boy's nostrils flare with a strange excitement, perhaps with a primitive recognition that he is returning to his first home. We pause before plunging. The boy's tiny fingers grasp my thumb, his perfect nails like small pink shells. My grandparents, the boy's great-grandparents, came to this land by crossing the same ocean. My wife's grandparents did the same. We were all made from their love—and from water.

We plunge, his green eyes wide, his red hair wet with spray. We are engulfed by sacred water. It is filled with the prayers of ten thousand shipwrecked souls, pleading to their gods in one hundred languages. We come up from the water, our faces stinging. The sea lies all around us. We have returned to Oceanus, to the great ocean-river, like an ever-flowing stream with no beginning and no end.

I hold the boy close to my chest. I press his cheek against my lips. The taste is familiar. It is the same as his mother's tears the day the miracle first dawned.

Geography of the Soul

Homo solus aut deus aut daemon
A solitary person is either a god or a demon

Robert Burton
The Anatomy of Melancholy

I have come to wonder if there is not a deep affinity between each of us and some particular kind of landscape. We would do well, I should think, to find out as soon as possible what kind it is. And we must be equally adept at discovering when the contours of that landscape begin to shift, for that change is usually indicative of a larger metamorphosis within.

I have begun this evening to think of the relationship of geography to the soul as I sit on the windswept wooden porch about thirty yards from the dune line. This evening the wind could blow the hair off a dog. The fine-grained dune stretched out before me is dotted with scraggly saw grass that quivers with emotion. Closer to the top of the dune, the grass bends back against the violent wind like the Indian Rubber Man pressed back by the sheer force of a gale.

Beyond the sand, but still close to the shore, the sea churns its steel gray water into ephemeral whitecaps. The waves come into unexpected existence and are then flattened by the wind to oblivion.

Farther out, larger waves clash as if doing the bidding of two opposed but unknowable sea gods. Above the horizon, enormous clouds, all in varying shades of foreboding gray, drift and mingle. For as long as I can remember this has been my landscape of choice. A great northeastern storm off the Atlantic coast has always stirred in me the deepest kinds of emotions—things primal and dark. When I begin to describe these storms I find myself reverting, in a curious way, to descriptions of the past turmoils in my soul. For much of life I have searched for an eye in these storms. It is only recently, in marriage and fatherhood, that I have found anything resembling a safe harbor.

This evening I am transfixed by the ferocity of it all. The power of the sea moves me with emotion that I am only beginning to understand. The years before my marriage were mostly lonely ones. I had friends and family, but found no one more companionable than what I thought was solitude. In his *Epistolae Morales* , Seneca, a first-century Roman philosopher, suggests that the primary sign of a well-ordered mind is a person's ability to remain in one place and to linger in his own company. But I have only recently understood that one can linger so long with only the mind as a companion until loneliness begins to be mistaken for solitude. It is then that the solitary life can become a dangerous life.

In *Death in Venice,* Thomas Mann writes that the solitary life may give birth to the original: to beauty, unfamiliar and perilous. But he warns that being alone might also bring forth the opposite: the perverse, illicit, and absurd. This is what happens to Mann's central character, Gustav von Aschenbach, a man who narrowed his life just to contain his art, while trying to deny the need for "the other," for companionship.

Wordsworth in the *Prelude* talks of being "parted from our better selves by the hurrying world." He takes for granted that we all know solitude is needed to find an authentic self. But he does not seem to entertain the possibility in his writings that one great peril in remaining too solitary is that we may lose our better self completely, for if it is never shared, then it is never tested by another better self. Yet in his life he seems to have understood this well.

This evening as I stare at the sheer power of the sea, my mind is like a kite set off in a great wind. In the past, my tether has too often seemed a flimsy string. I have always worried about it breaking, leaving me adrift and perhaps to plunge into a foreboding sea. But this evening I know the lines that secure me to the earth, my son and his mother, and another baby growing in her womb, are much more secure than all my former solitude ever had promised. My inner landscape is rapidly changing. The sea within me flattens out. My kite happily and irrevocably becomes entangled in the lines of others, and yet it miraculously remains in flight.

In his *Pensées,* seventeenth-century French philosopher Blaise Pascal offers the opinion that "all misery comes from one thing: not knowing how to remain alone." But this evening with the gentle light fading and my inner landscape too transformed to resemble any longer the ferocity stretched before me, I know that a good part of life's misery also comes in knowing too well how to be alone. It has taken me half a lifetime to discover the many benefits of solitude. Clearly one of these is a simple apprehension of a sweet need for the other.

Music is its Roar

He that will learn to pray, let him go to the sea.

Scottish proverb

It is not often I have a genuine sense of place, an experience of something fine and good that comes solely from where I am, not what or who I have become. There are many forms of homelessness. There are many ways to be disenfranchised, evicted from one's place in things. I am lucky enough to suffer only intermittently from a metaphysical variety of placelessness.

I sit this evening on a small wooden porch that juts out above the dune line. Clumps of grass, dotting the sand like sparse strands of hair clinging to a bald man's head, can no longer be seen. The small driftwood-colored rabbits who inhabit the dunes have disappeared for the evening.

Earlier in the day when the sun was high, I watched as a pair of four-year-old boys, looking like two small King Canutes, threw wads of wet sand at the onrushing surf. The great sea paid little notice to the boys. Just a little farther off shore, about ten yards apart, porpoises broke the surface almost simultaneously, one, two, three, four, five, then gone again. Thirty seconds later, they reappeared, noses and shinning dorsal fins surfacing first, followed by a great arching and five choreographed dives into one watery disappearance.

But this evening everything has disappeared. I write with the aid of a small oil lamp found while rummaging in the kitchen of this rented house. The lamp provides just enough light to see the ruled paper's faint blue lines running parallel to the invisible horizon.

Stretched out before me is a darkness that cannot be found in the city. Beyond the dunes, beyond the crickets sounding like the monotonous hum of high-tension wires, at the very edge of the earth, the ancient sea unfolds itself and then slowly gathers itself in again. The slowly building cadence, followed by the sudden crash of waves, is like no other sound. This evening, while my family sleeps and I am left alone with the lamp and my No. 2 pencil, no metaphor seems worthy of it.

I have been here now for nearly an hour, thinking and listening. A moment ago, I remembered a line from Byron that has started me writing. He speaks of "a society where none intrudes by the deep sea, and music is its roar." These are words written at night, by this same great ocean. Lord Byron has been dead since 1824, and yet we share this same experience.

Tomorrow the newspapers once again will bring me the comings and goings of men of action: a war waits to happen in the Middle East; gasoline prices on the rise; and a late baseball game played 3,000 miles away. But this evening, the great sea drowns out all in its wide sound. The noise cleanses me. It is like a baptism. It imposes a rhythm upon everything visible and invisible. In the darkness the sound and smell of the sea seems to make the spiritual possible.

Ancient Hindu priests in their scriptures, the *Upanisads* and the *Bramanas*, depicted the merging of individuals' souls with ultimate reality, Brahma, as drops splashing in a dark and vast sea. The sound they made, the sages said, was like a great wave crashing. Charles Darwin thought our deep fascination with the sea comes from a kind of racial memory of our oceanic origins, a time before men of action set out to conquer the land and each other. Freud believed the great rhythm of the sea reminds us all of the womb's salt sea, a place well protected from men of action.

In a few days, back in the city, my students will bring clean spiral notebooks and freshly sharpened No. 2 pencils to my classroom. They and I, once again, will be very diligent. We will read together works by men who lived by the sea: Thales, Anaximander, Plato, Aristotle, and Seneca. In one of my lectures, just before the ancient trees on campus again give up their leaves for dead, I will loosen my tie, lean on the podium and speak earnestly about Plato's conception of immortality. And then I will tell them about this evening. I will tell them about how just beyond the darkness, with a starless night and a cool breeze blowing from the west, the sea sounded and smelled like eternity.

Seeing Clearly in the Dark

God made beauties in nature like a child playing in the sand.

Apollonius of Tyana
Fragments

Childhood sometimes pay a second visit to a man; youth never.

Ana Jameson
Letters

In the fading evening light, in that time before all turns gray, then black, anything can happen. This evening with the great sea stretched out just beyond the dune grass, a small rabbit with fur the color of wet sand begins to make his way across the dunes and into a backyard marked off by leaning snow fences, the pickets battered and faded pink by winter storms.

Earlier in the week at twilight my five-year-old son and I first spotted the rabbit coming out of his thicket. The boy wanted to know who owned the bunny. Then he ran into the house, tore open the refrigerator door, liberating a small carrot for our cotton-tailed visitor. By the time the child returned the rabbit had wisely disappeared. But now in the dying light he has returned. He watches me with caution, and then finally decides he will not find a meal here. A moment later he moves on to the high grass just atop the dune line and vanishes.

Closer to the ocean, what is left of the sun casts long shadows across a deserted beach. The last of a flock of hungry sea gulls glide to the edge of the surf, searching for what few morsels are given up by the tumbling surf. The birds fight each other for territory, but there is little of sustenance to be found here and they move farther down the beach.

A while later, the sun disappears and I begin to feel the bites of mosquitoes. Then comes the sound of a "minor nation" of crickets. Their song always comes as an afterthought. Like the sound of the sea, the crickets chirping goes unnoticed until we attend to it, making it all the sound there is. There are some parts of life that sit unobtrusively on the edge of consciousness until they formally are invited in: the electric sound of crickets; the creaking sounds of an old house; or the distant hum of a refrigerator motor heard in the middle of a sleepless night.

Still later, a solid cloud cover rolls in turning the sky velvet black. Away from the city lights, darkness becomes real darkness. The boy and I walk quietly along the sand, our small flashlight combing the crevices looking for sand crabs. The one-armed diggers wait patiently in the sand burrows until the last fading light, and then they climb to freedom, searching for what the gulls may have left behind. In the daylight they quietly live beneath beach chairs and spread blankets smelling of coconut oil. But in the dark, with the small flashlight providing shadow and light, they inhabit a world that looks more like the surface of the moon.

Behind the small drama of the sand crabs' appearances and retreats is the sound of a now invisible sea. It gathers itself in and then crashes, creating strange phosphorescent ripples against a black satin background. In his book of meditations titled *The Christian Virtuoso*, seventeenth-century philosopher and scientist Robert Boyle speaks of nature as a fine tapestry rolled up, so that we are never able to see the whole of it at once. We must be content, he says, to wait for its beauty and symmetry to unfold in its own time. Some elements of the tapestry work silently, like the furtive actions of the sand crabs. They come into being and possess very little. They fulfill their function in the larger work in progress, and then they return as silently as they came. The pattern constitutes an eternal law. The law unfolds itself, as the tapestry does, in a great rhythm—a rhythm that sometimes can be seen most clearly in the dark. It is an eternal law as real as the invisible sea.

Readers of Messages

When anxious, uneasy and bad thoughts come, I go to the sea,
and the sea drowns them out with its great wide sounds,
cleanses me with its noise and imposes a rhythm upon
everything in me that is bewildered and confused.

Rainer Maria Rilke
Letters 1892-1910

We human beings see things in fire. To gaze into the glowing
heat is to gaze into the light: the fire is a magic crystal.
It helps us to see visions and to dream dreams.

Holbrook Jackson
Southward Ho! And Other Essays

It is late afternoon. Seagulls hang against a scarlet sunset like iridescent crosses. For an instant they offer a silent thanksgiving, a benediction for this day full of sun and grace. Finally, they swoop down to the sand, competing for crumbs dropped by a toddler and his eight-year-old brother.

First there were two, then seven, a moment later seventeen, until eventually the small boy has thirty-two hungry seagulls watching his every move. Their wings come precariously near, but they never collide, each bird with its own air-traffic controller buried deep within its tiny skull, a gift of evolutionary biology and perhaps the hand of God.

The small boy's hands move as if he is conducting an orchestra. For the moment he seems to command the waves, and the birds, and the sand. He stands at the shore waving his arms like a self-confident King Canute, the Scandinavian king who foolishly attempted to command the ocean waves to stop. The boy has more than enough time remaining to understand his more complex relationship to the natural world.

The father's heart yearns to find secret messages in all this: in the scent of sea air, the disappearing sun, the curve of his wife's back as she bends to assist the boy, the slow advance and retreat of the ocean, its "great wide sound," and in the silences left between the waves. In this place it is not difficult to imagine why Thales and Anaximander, two ancient Greek philosophers, believed that all life, all love, comes from the sea. We are the great readers of messages: we see things in the water.

Later in the evening, the father is alone on the porch. Dishes have been washed, sunburns attended to, bedtime stories told. His wife sleeps soundly, a reward of sorts for chasing the little boy all day on the beach. The man stops in the doorway to admire her new freckles. She even sleeps gracefully.

The sea is invisible now. As its roar changes to a low moan, the man's thoughts turn to a one-legged seagull seen earlier in the day. The man stares at the flame of a citronella candle, wondering if the bird must remain in constant flight. The man wonders why this bird, and not another? He remembers it was Heraclitus, "the weeping philosopher," who believed all has come from fire and must someday return to it.

A moment later a moth begins to circle the flame. It becomes dizzy, drunk with attraction, and finally dives into the light, losing its wings and legs immediately. Seconds later, the wax rises covering his abdomen and head, and the moth becomes a second wick. The man stares for several minutes at the twin sources of light. He thinks of those Medieval mystics who described their love for God as a burning wick in the midst of a divine flame. But the man also remembers those Buddhist monks in Southeast Asia who sacrificed themselves as protest against the Vietnam war. Human wicks with faces contorted in their final act of self-immolation. We are great readers of messages: we see things in fire.

This is, of course, the question: what should we see in water or fire? It was raised by writer Annie Dillard and a self-immolating moth on a wintry island in the Puget sound: "Faith would be, in short, that God has willful connection with time whatsoever, and with us." Pope's answer was that "all Nature is but Art." Wordsworth, in Book I of the *Prelude*, gives the same response:

> Dust, as we are, the immortal spirit grows
> Like harmony in music, there is a dark
> Inscrutable workmanship that reconciles
> Discordant elements.

We cannot know. We can only believe. The rest is waiting—waiting for crumbs dropped by the hand of a caring, but sometimes distant, God.

Time and Habit

The present moment is significant, not as a bridge between past and future, but by reason of its contents, which can fill our emptiness and become ours, it we are capable of receiving them.

Dag Hammarskjold
Markings

It is midnight, an enchanted moment when one day disappears and another mysteriously springs from its ruins. It is that portion of the night that John Milton wisely labeled "the noon of thought." I sit with borrowed paper and pencil at a kitchen table. Outside the window, a gentle breeze moves through a South Carolina palm tree, while a lone, low-country lizard slowly makes its way along a white wooden porch railing.

It is a curious fact that a dramatic change of place often has the effect of allowing one to see time in a new way. A change of scene destroys habit, like a giant cable unwinding one strand at a time. Back home, against the backdrop of our regular life, these habitual threads are too small to be seen or felt, but they slowly combine, day after day, until they are too strong to be broken.

Earlier in the day, I walked with family and friends a half mile out into a vanished ocean. Low tide had made the great Atlantic recede a few thousand feet, revealing its ocean bed. Tiny tidal pools, no deeper than the length of my index finger formed little lakes between mounds of silt. It gave the visitors the feeling of being giants who had happened upon the Egyptian Sahara just moments after the Nile had burst over its banks. We had arrived at the proper time.

We hopped from island to island, examining the few small hermit crabs left by the great sea. They lay in the shallow pools, looking at first like small encrusted stones, or perhaps barnacles dropped from an ancient vessel.

For an hour or so we moved along the ocean floor, four small children and three adults acting like children. A while later, the tide began to change, and my wife wisely cautioned us to return to the security of the shore, and the confinement of our shoes. My wife is good at thinking about the future, and finding the dangers that might be lurking there. She is the responsible member of our family. I am more infatuated with the past. Neither of us thinks enough about the present. In our regular life, the one that races on back home, we always have some place to go. Often my wife points me in the proper direction, or, when necessary, gently tries to drag me behind her.

This evening I am thinking about how little appreciation we have for the present. We are like the ancient Roman worshippers of Janus, the god of all beginnings, and the root of our word "January." Janus was usually depicted with two faces, one peering out at the past, the other focusing on the future. But Janus had no eye on the present. Perhaps the Romans were as uncomfortable with the present as we seem to be. Like us, they lived at various distances from it. Fears, hopes, and habits make the present an uninhabitable place.

The present can only be seen, of course, when moving at the proper speed. On the plane ride back to our regular life, we will cover a distance of over 500 miles in less than an hour. But this evening, things move at a slower pace, and I am suddenly reminded of the ancient Greek festival to the god Pan, the giver of children and happiness. At the feast of Pan, the Athenians held a foot race, all the competitors bearing torches. The first runner to appear at the shrine was declared the winner. With his medal came the promise of happiness and fecundity. But it was rarely the swiftest afoot who won the prize. If one ran too fast, the torch was extinguished by the wind, instantly disqualifying the competitor. If a runner were too slow, his torch oil did not last long enough to reach the sacred destination.

The Greeks thought that happiness could only be gained by moving at the right speed. This is why they were the inventors of the story of the tortoise and the hare. And it is why they made an important distinction between *kronos*, time measured in discrete units, time lost and saved, and *kairos*, the right time—a distinction not preserved in the English language. With *kairos* we understand the difference between accident and grace. It is the kind of time kept on the marriage bed and at the death bed. It was *kairos* that brought us poetry, while *kronos* brought us compound interest, call-waiting, and the fax machine.

Darkness Visible

No light but rather darkness visible.

John Milton
Paradise Lost I

Longfellow was taking poetic license when he wrote, "The day is done and darkness falls from the wings of night." Night does not fall. It rises.

L.J. & M.J. Milne
The World of Night

The sun's upper rim drops beneath the great sea. Off on the distant horizon the ocean appears to have caught fire. Where the sea meets sky all is purple, then, a few moments later, the light on the horizon begins to fade. A half an hour later, all light has been squeezed from the edge of the earth. The day has been spent in heavy cloud cover, the sun only making itself visible in its retreat. This evening there will be no stars. The sky is bible black, like the void before creation.

Standing alone on the beach, the darkness finally has gathered. It came creeping in like a frightened black cat. The ancient writer Hesiod gave darkness the name "mother of the gods," for the Greeks believed that before anything existed, there was darkness everywhere. The people of the Maiana islands in the Pacific, a place devoid of artificial lights until the 1940s, have four different words for the varying degrees of darkness. The most sacred of these is "Po," the void out of which all things come.

Among the Tuamotu islanders, the god Kihu dwells in a black, gleamless realm, out of which all life magically springs. Like the writers of the Hebrew bible, the Tuamotuans believe the first thing God created was light. In Tuamotu mythology creation occurs through speech. Light leaps out of the darkness of Kihu's mouth. The seas are made from divine saliva.

But darkness has not meant simply creation for *homo sapiens.* Like the creator god of Abraham, Isaac, and Jacob, one of the first and most impressive of human inventions is fire. It was not simply for cooking. It was also to chase away the darkness. Human beings have always had an ambivalent relationship with the darkness. As children few of us were able to master our fear of the dark. Even now I take a deep breath before descending alone to the basement. And yet the darkness is our first and last home. We move from the darkness of the womb to the darkness of the grave. In the time between, we are mostly afraid of the dark.

It is curious that when we do not know something, we say we are in the dark. The boogeyman lives in the dark, as does that Thing beneath the bed. Darkness was the abode of Pluto, the most fearful of the Greek gods. Kierkegaard spoke of the loss of faith as the dark night of the soul. In *Leaves of Grass*, Walt Whitman makes sisters of death and darkness. And yet, when darkness takes sight away, it so often provides those eyes within us. These unseen eyes are so unpredictable. They provide a seamless background, as they do this evening, for making sense out of the self.

Darkness forces thought inward. It often brings strange fears and longings. Sometimes it resurrects the dead. More than anything, darkness often demands an accounting of the self. As I walk along this deserted beach, the darkness asks what I am doing with my life. I attempt a few feeble responses.

A few moments later, I come upon a flood-lit beach. Children are playing with a Frisbee. The sphere is thrown far out into the darkness. The three boys look to each other to see who will retrieve it. They decide they will find it in the morning, and they head back on the wooden walkway toward the lights of home. But I move beyond the flood light, and a few moments later I am back in the darkness, moving among the invisible.

A Circle So Wide

The huge concentric waves of universal life are shoreless. The starry sky that we study is but partial appearance. We grasp but a few measures of the vast network of existence.

Victor Hugo
William Shakespeare

We have returned to this small cottage by the great sea. The regularity of the tide's advances and retreats, and the sun's daily journey from east to west, almost convince me that things at the beach do not change. Each day the sun begins as a faint hint of pink on the eastern horizon. In moments, it becomes a fiery red ball, emerging from beneath shining beveled glass. As it dies in the evening, it illuminates the western sky in colors that defy adequate description. All this happens with daily regularity. It is predictable, and thus it seems changeless.

This year's lifeguard knows he has muscles, as did last year's lifeguard. His girlfriend spends the day beneath his stand. (Last year, I remember, that lifeguard's girlfriend claimed the same spot.) She is blonde and beautiful. She smells of baby oil and innocence, as she always has. Back in the city, I manage to exude a patina of political correctness, but here by the sea there is still the secret stir of testosterone when the right woman makes her way up the beach. I look just long enough to trigger that amused side-glance my wife uses to watch me watch them.

In late afternoon, the sandpipers and gulls still spread their hieroglyphic tracks across the sand, as they have for all the summers we have come to this place. The Greeks gave us the modern name for the ancient religious language of the Egyptians. "Hieroglyphics" meant "sacred carvings," which were only used to describe the eternal, changeless world of the gods.

The sea and salt air still heal minor cuts and abrasions faster than any medicine found in the city. The surf always manages to work its magic on our more secret wounds as well.

The beach in evening time is still the domain of feisty mosquitoes that wait patiently in the marshes until the sun sets. And the stars continue to spread themselves blazing across the firmament, as they have since the first days of creation.

Our cottage remains bereft of a decent spaghetti colander or six matching wine glasses. The same folks line up for the Sunday paper at the small shop in town. The paper brings news of a world where things change too quickly and too clearly. But here, if one does not think too much, the world is predictable, perhaps even eternal.

After a few days, though, the notion that this is a changeless place gradually fades, like the ever-shortening summer light. There are many clues that this place will not guarantee eternal life: a pelican's swift and deadly plunge for an evening meal; the vacant shells of horseshoe crabs washed ashore, like the forgotten helmets of soldiers long since drowned at sea; an enormous gray speckled fish head tumbled ashore, the eyes missing from its sockets, gill bones exposed on one side.

In moments, the dead fish draws a crowd. A dozen people reverently, quietly surround its head. As the stiff-armed lifeguard carries it off, an older woman, lips ringed with zinc oxide, comments to no one in particular that the lifeguard is a brave young man.

Seeing the old woman reminds me that the ocean is a great cemetery, no different than Forest Lawn and Arlington National Cemetery that hold so many of our war dead. The appearance of the horseshoe crab shells and the fish revive in me thoughts of my uneasy relationship with the dead. I continually struggle to find a meeting ground with the dead. I am not usually successful. I cannot treat the dead as if they are truly and wholly dead, for that would reveal a want of affection and possibility. And yet, I cannot treat the dead as fully among the living, for that would imply a denial of time that only the very young so effortlessly achieve.

Later in the week, the beach again transforms me. This is not a place where the immortal can be found. During the first few days here, I tried, in my own way, to deny the passage of time. In order to achieve that goal, I needed to agree to not think too much. A tumbling fish head, however, changed me.

I began to look more closely at this place, our place by the great sea. My nine-year-old son no longer holds my hand when he enters the surf. His two-year-old brother still will not venture very far into the churning ocean. Last year, he barley spoke at all; now he calls the treacherous current the "undertoad" and the protective skin lotion "sun scream."

It is not long until everything about this place whispers a language of finitude, and I finally understand that the time I tried to deny was of the linear variety. But here, by the sea, I discover that time moves in a great circle—a circle so wide that it cannot be apprehended by a single soul. I understand that this place is not much different from any place: the dead are always holding hands with the living.

Chapter

Two

On Rites of Passage

Today is not yesterday. We ourselves change. How then can our works and thoughts, if they are always to be the fittest, continue always the same—change, indeed is painful, yet ever needful; and if memory have its force and worth, so also has hope.

Thomas Carlyle

I long have been fascinated by rites of passage: the movement from darkness to light, from ignorance to knowledge, from innocence to the sometimes painful world of experience. In our culture we do a very poor job of marking and making these passages. Adulthood in America is marked by something spit out of a computer at the department of motor vehicles. Death often comes when we decide to flip the switch off on a respirator. In this second chapter, I try to make some sense of a few of the most important, and thus the most holy, of these transitions.

Is It Over Yet?

Let us all watch well our beginnings.

Alexander Clark
Letters

The game isn't over till it's over.

Yogi Berra
NBC Interview
September 5, 1971

My wife thinks I spend too much time in the shower. Sometimes I can sense her sneaking nervously into the bathroom to make sure I have not fractured my skull by stepping on a misplaced bar of deodorant soap. This morning I could feel her lurking out there in the steam, wondering if it would be prudent to tap the opaque sliding door before she moved it along its little aluminum track, so that she might properly identify the body. I really should tell her I take these long showers because they are among the only events in my life where the beginning and the end are so clearly defined.

I don't remember when I began having this problem of deciding when things begin or end. I think it began when my maternal grandfather died a few months before my fifth birthday, though, as I said, I'm not really certain about these matters. He used to sit in an overstuffed green reclining chair. He always read books without any pictures. Sometimes, in the midst of reading, he would stop and notice me. Then he would put his hand deep in his pleated trousers and pull out pennies for me. Then, one day, he died. I was too young to read Gilbert Chesterton. He could have told me that the trouble with the last time is that we so rarely know it is the last time. After my grandfather died, I continued to look for him in the green reclining chair with the broken wooden lever. I thought he must still be there, only smaller. I don't know how or when I decided to no longer look for him.

I know this problem about discovering the beginning and end of things was already a great difficulty when I was on my summer vacation between the first and second grades. I think the nuns could not decide on whether I had passed or not. I believe they told my mother they would wait and see. They left blank the little box marked "promoted to grade two" on the back of my manila-colored report card.

In the heat of summer, with my mother's mouth full of wooden clothes pins, and her attention turned toward hanging my father's enormous, pitch-covered work clothes out to dry, I would sneak into the drawer filled with dead flashlights, faded Polaroid photographs and important family papers. I would stare at the back of my report card and wonder just when the first grade would come to an end.

That same summer, I remember my mother telling me, sometime in early June, that I could stay out to play until it got dark. I remember sitting on the hill behind Johnny Hucke's house, with the twilight gathering. I thought to myself, "Is this real darkness?" and then, a moment later, "No, maybe this is darkness." Deeper into the heart of summer it was more than a minor consolation to me that the fireflies seemed to share my confusion.

In September, I lined up for school with the new first-graders, but the good sisters, without any help from me, had somehow decided over the summer that I had the stuff for the second grade, so they sent me along to mass with my former classmates. I figured somewhere in my permanent record—the one the FBI might come along and want to look at someday—some very official School Sister of Notre Dame had checked the all-important box on the back of my first report card. But I marveled, even then, about how the anonymous woman could be so sure.

Back then, I had the hardest time knowing when I was in or out of trouble. When I was about eight years old my mother bought a little wooden wall-hanging marked "The Vicchios' Dog House." Beneath the simple white A-frame doghouse hung an assortment of tiny canines each marked with the first name of my parents or one of their children. The object was for one of the Vicchio pooches always to occupy the A-frame. I had little difficulty in understanding how my mother knew when to put me in the doghouse, but it was always a genuine mystery how she decided just when to return my little Dalmatian to its silver hook.

Many years later, I became an adult. I don't know when or where it happened. These are difficult matters to decide in a culture where one's only rites of passage are supplied by the Motor Vehicle Administration and the Liquor Board. At what moment did I cease to be a child? And when did my parents have the good sense to stop treating me as one? At which Archimedean point did the world tilt and my mistakes become mine alone?

I know now that I am deep into adulthood. But I am not sure yet if I am middle-aged. My jump shot is going. And I can't remember the names of my graduate-school classmates—people to whom, over beers at a bar called Rudy's, I pledged my undying loyalty.

Now, many years later, this problem with the beginning and end of things seems no better. I do not know how bald babies decide it's time to be born and bald tires decide it's time to blow out. I don't know how crickets know it's over. How do cocks decide when the farmers have had too much sleep? These birds have a cranial capacity about the size of a walnut, but they seem to know when.

I know that hope comes like a cold and leaves like a thief. It always seems to go just when one's attention is turned the other way. It is difficult to comprehend when love comes, or more importantly, when it departs. Emily Dickinson, with rather uncharacteristic boldness, declares, "Love can do all but raise the dead." But how could she be so sure?

This incapacity on my part to know the precise origins and ends of things, of course, now has dramatic repercussions. My profession as a teacher of philosophy requires me more times than not to reside in what Henry James has aptly called "the Province of the Great Perhaps." I don't know the moment when life begins, though people on both sides of the debate seem to be so sure about the matter. And I am not at all certain when life comes to a close. I wonder whether the soul doesn't sometimes linger in the mortal shell for one more touch, one breath, one final word before that eternal sameness, the end that some say ends all ends.

A Rite of (Bus) Passage

You cannot acquire experience by making experiments.
You cannot create experience. You must undergo it.

Albert Camus
Notebooks 1935-42

The boy's first day of school: I thought it would be one of those unforgettably poignant moments, the kind of experience one files away in some special region of memory so that it might be retrieved for some important purpose later in his life.

The bus was to come at 7:55. We were to meet in the front of the SuperFresh. During the short ride to the supermarket parking lot, I had imagined I'd have a pep talk with the six-year-old. That tiny script writer/director inside my skull had the father talking to the son about making new friends, about paying careful attention to the teacher, and about the importance of having fun.

In the script in my head I told the boy about how at his age I walked a mile and a half to my West Baltimore grade school, usually in the snow. In a very poignant close-up I told the boy about how I took off my shoes and walked in bare feet so I could save shoe leather. At the end of the scene I imagined the boy's tear-stained face pressed up against the back window of the bus, as the fumes from the yellow

Leviathan brought a glisten to the father's eyes.

The actual send-off looked more like a production of *Aida*—without the elephants. By 7:45 the SuperFresh's parking lot was crowded with an assortment of vehicles in which my wife, her mother, her father, my sister-in-law, my nine-year-old niece, and a close family friend had traveled to witness this important rite of bus passage. They all brought cameras.

By 7:50 the people preparing for the day's work inside the SuperFresh were staring in our direction. It looked to them for all the world as though a six-year-old in khaki shorts and a blue blazer was holding a press conference in front of the store.

You could see the man who runs the produce department and a couple of checkers mouthing the words, "Who is that boy?" They must have thought that in the midst of all their royal troubles, one of Prince Charles' and Lady Di's sons had gone missing and somehow mysteriously reappeared at a suburban Baltimore supermarket.

The bus appeared on time. Holding his parents' hands, the boy coolly walked the few paces to the open door. He swung into the first seat and didn't look back. It was as if he had already made most of the 3,420 trips he will take before starting college.

And yet, he didn't know how un-cool it is to sit in the seat behind the driver. There was something about the juxtaposition of his confident facade and the innocence of his sitting in the first seat that reminded me of just how irrevocably changed the boy was about to become. Watching the tail-lights of the bus pull away that first day began a curious kind of grief in me.

Until now, the boy has been filled with the most extraordinary capacity to wonder, and with wonder came truth. He has run headlong into his young life, but he has not always found those truths in the places where his new school, or any school to come, will suggest he look.

I have not taught my son well enough that there are places where joy is not so easily found. He has not learned that exuberance is not always a virtue, or that cruelty comes more easily than tenderness for some people.

I don't think he will learn these unfortunate things at his new school. But the school is surely symbolic of a world that cannot be as well-ordered and easily orchestrated as the sheltered one in which he has lived for his first six years.

A few weeks ago, we ran together through the summer rain in nothing more than our undershorts. That day, I pressed him close to my chest. I held him so tightly, I could feel his heart beating. I remember thinking that day that this will not last long. These imperceptible moments of innocence vanish. They change so subtly. The changes add up, gradually becoming something larger until early childhood becomes an entire life.

As the bus pulled away from the SuperFresh, I remembered the boy sitting at the beach as a three-year-old. He placed dry sand in a sieve and watched intently as it drained back onto the beach. After a while, I placed some wet sand in the sieve so that it might trap the handfuls he placed in it. The boy was amazed. It was as if somehow I had slowed time. The boy thought I knew magic. I wish I did.

When Joy and Suffering Converge

Sorrow makes us all children again.

Oscar Wilde
De Profundis

There is something about profound joy and suffering that has a way of collapsing space and time.

I was recently reminded of this truism. I stood along with friends, family, and members of a large reform congregation in Northwest Baltimore, as the thirteen-year-old daughter of close friends read the *haftorah* as part of her bat mitzvah.

The girl's voice was clear and surprisingly strong, as she read the Hebrew of Leviticus and Ezekiel. Afterward, as part of her prayer, the girl remarked that her parents had added an "a" to her first name to honor the memory of Anne Frank. In 1945, one month after her thirteenth birthday, Annelies Marie Frank went into hiding with her family in the back rooms of her father's food products business in Amsterdam. Three years later Anne Frank died of typhus at the Bergen-Belsen concentration camp near Hanover, Germany.

If Anne Frank were alive today, she would be in her mid-sixties. She would be about the same age as the proud grandmothers of the bat mitzvah girl. Instead, space and time are frozen for Anne Frank.

She will forever remain a girl.

I thought about Anne Frank for the rest of the Sabbath service. When it came time to read the *kaddish*, the Jewish prayer of mourning, I found myself standing with members of bereaved families, clumsily reciting the Aramaic prayer in the ancient Hebrew I had tried to master in graduate school.

Later, my wife asked me why I stood at the reciting of the *kaddish*. She knew that under normal circumstances, only Jews read the prayer, and only those who mourn. I did not know at the time why I stood.

The next morning, while reading the newspaper, I understood why I became a mourner at the service. Joy and sorrow have a way of putting effects before their causes.

In Berlin, in what may be called the last Nazi trial in Germany, Josef Schwammberger, the former head of a forced labor camp, was sentenced to life in prison for killing thirty-four people and participating in the deaths of hundreds of others. (Schwammberger was believed to have participated in 3,377 deaths, but he was tried only for those killings for which there are living witnesses.)

Schwammberger, now a gaunt and bent-up eighty-year-old man, had pleaded not guilty to the charges. During his brief testimony he said that he could not remember what he had done as an SS officer.

Other memories were much better, much clearer. Nearly 100 witnesses catalogued a series of atrocities that caused people to call Schwammberger "the god of life and death." Among the crimes for which Schwammberger was convicted was the murder of a rabbi, identified only as Fraenkel, on September 21, 1942. The rabbi had refused to work on Yom Kippur, the holiest of Jewish holidays. Other testimony implicated Josef Schwammberger in the 1942 murder of a thirteen-year-old girl whose skull was crushed because the commandant did not want to waste a bullet. That girl, too, would be in her sixties had she not been frozen in space and time.

I know now that I stood at the reading of the *kaddish* because Anne Frank no longer has a family member to pray for her. Her mother died at Auschwitz in 1945, her sister at Bergen-Belsen in the same year. Her father was found hospitalized at Auschwitz when its horrors were revealed by Russian troops. Otto Frank died in 1980 after a life of devotion to the memory of his vanished family. I do not know if any of the other girl's family survived the holocaust. I stood in case they had not.

Anne Frank was no different from the thirteen-year-old bat mitzvah girl who bravely stood at the podium and, in clear and haunting Hebrew, expressed her faith. Both those girls are no different from the unnamed thirteen-year-old whose precious life was bludgeoned from her because a madman in Germany thought a bullet was too good for her.

The rabbis officiating at the coming-of-age service were no different from their brave predecessor, Fraenkel, who refused to make a mockery of the day of atonement. Time and space collapsed for me that morning, and I only barely understood enough to stand for the *kaddish*.

These peoples' faces are blurred together for me. I cannot tell where one face begins and another ends. They are all part of being Jewish. They are all wrapped together in joy and sorrow. They were all there for dancing and the celebration after the bat mitzvah, as surely as the two proud grandmothers were.

The combination of such profound joy at the accomplishments of my thirteen-year-old friend, and the deep sorrow at the mention of Anne Frank, had made me stand that morning. As I write this, I cannot get out of my head the image of Anne Frank, of Rabbi Fraenkel, of that anonymous thirteen-year-old girl. I keep thinking about what the terror must have been like. I keep thinking of them frozen together forever.

Hannah Arendt once remarked that joy is something one participates in with others, while suffering more often happens alone. I think this aphorism does not fit Jewish suffering. The Jewish people so often have had to find small currents of joy in a black sea of suffering. They have been forced to find great joy together because so often extraordinary suffering has been thrust upon them as a group. I saw a glimpse of that realization on the faces of the elderly in that Baltimore synagogue.

I stood there because none of us should ever forget. I stood there the other morning because the faces had become one. I stood because suffering was wrapped around this great moment of joy like a nut in its shell. And for that moment I understood something of what it must mean to be a Jew.

Autumnal Universes

Then summer fades and passes, and October comes.
We'll smell smoke then, and feel an unsuspected sharpness,
a thrill of nervous, swift elation, a sense of sadness and departure.

Thomas Wolfe
You Can't Go Home Again

One morning, in the world we must often refer to as the real one, I heard that a very important Iranian ayatollah has pronounced a death sentence on Arabs and Israelis alike who are participating in the Mideast peace talks. It seems to the ayatollah that the best way to bring peace to the troubled region is to kill any Jew or Arab who might sit down to talk about it. I thought that Alice's Red Queen probably is not even out of bed yet, but it will be a day she surely will find to her liking.

When I begin to have thoughts like these, I usually find my way to the back of our property, through old trees I know well but whose names I have never learned. And so this morning I passed through the gate on my way to some alternative universes.

On the path, just past the first clump of trees, I found the blue bones of a rabbit, picked clean by a swarm of ants. A few moments later, I could feel the warmth of the sun working its way into my hair.

But in another instant, a cloud covered the sun, and a bitter little wind found me alone among the hollies. Archibald Alison, a little-known but very wise Scottish divine, once began an essay on November with this query: "Who at this season does not feel impressed with a sentiment of melancholy?"

The woods are, of course, a mostly simple place. At this time of year much of the life there is doing its dying. On even the most cursory of walks in the autumnal quiet, something takes form, something Keats came to understand by looking at an urn. Unmistakably, perhaps irretrievably, we are all partly made of leaves and vegetable mold.

Reveries, as well as universes, begin and end very quickly in the woods. A spider travels like a thief up an invisible thread. I follow the tiny creature's progress until I come to the glistening web. I touch it gently with a twig. The silent motion instantly send signals to a tiny spider brain. His (or her) world is a tightly circumscribed one, but it holds real danger. In still another universe, a few paces away, drops from an evening shower have made tiny pools on leaves that will drop by nightfall.

Back in my world, the one I keep within, I think about how often I yearn for those things that are clearly finite. I try to remember the voice of a grandfather dead thirty-five years. I try to recall the smells, the sounds that made him real, but they are mostly lost. A moment later, I think about heading into winter. I think about how we all must find something tough and reliable, something that will outlast the darkness.

In winter, love must learn to roll itself into a ball, small and tight. It must stick close to the bone. It must be very patient, until it hears once again the murmuring of the earth. If resurrection is possible, it will come only after a long winter's night. The most difficult part of faith, I have come to learn, is trying to believe that even the longest of winters are not permanent. Back on the path, on the way out of the woods, I remember a Hindu tale of the god Krishna's mother. One day, while wiping the baby god's mouth, she inadvertently peered inside and beheld the universe.

I have walked in the woods enough now to ask which one.

Taking Leave

The melancholy days are come, the saddest of the year,
Of wailing winds, and naked woods, and meadows brown and sere.

William Cullen Bryant
The Death of Flowers

I teach ancient philosophy in the fall. When I arrive with my students at the work of Heraclitus, the leaves are giving themselves up and one can feel an unsuspected sharpness in the air, the first breaths of cold sweeping down from the north. Just about this time, I look out at the oaks that frame my classroom window and I tell my students that, among the ancient Greeks, Heraclitus was known as "the weeping philosopher" because he thought that only the transitory was real.

Heraclitus was preoccupied with what came to be known in the history of philosophy as the problem of change. He was the man who said one cannot step in the same river twice. He seems to have been overtaken by the sheer transitoriness of things. He knew that all of life is as ephemeral as a soap bubble in the mind of God. This autumn Heraclitus is on my mind. In this season of departure, two of my friends have taken life's leave. They will not see the leaves turn in another fall.

As far as I know, my two friends never met. They would not have had much in common had I introduced them. The woman was in the process of raising two boys. The man never married. The woman was a devout Catholic, the man ordained in the Presbyterian church. They did share the career of teaching—and a disease that took their lives too early.

But it is about their teaching I wish to tell you.

Like life, teaching is an ephemeral art. It is often done in out-of-the-way places, for not very much money, by people who only get their names in the newspaper when life's spark has left their bodies. Unlike the making of a book or the producing of a film, good teaching dissipates like smoke, or rather, we must depend on our students to carry our teaching silently in their hearts and minds.

Teachers, of course, always know who the good teachers are. We all secretly compare ourselves to each other. Both my friends were extraordinary teachers. The man built a reputation for kindness and scholarship as a teacher of Hebrew language and literature. The woman was an energetic and creative member of the business department at the College of Notre Dame.

Before the end, my friend wrote letters to her boys. She wrote about their particular gifts and aspirations, she tried to tell them some of the things they would need to hear after she was gone: that courage is a virtue that is not bestowed, but must be created daily; that fortitude, tenderness, and hope should never be in short supply.

The woman died a few days after being honored as the College's distinguished teacher of the year. I was on the committee that forwarded her name to the president. In the hours of meetings leading to the committee's selection, there was not one sentence uttered about her brain tumor. She was chosen because she was an extraordinary teacher. She regained consciousness long enough to know she had won the award, and then she died.

One winter, the man found out about his liver cancer. He struggled through surgery, various kinds of experimental chemotherapy, and the normal indignities we have come to expect in this age of advanced medicine. In the midst of his suffering, he decided to continue his plans to take his students to the Holy Land. By spring the disease had made great inroads. His weight was down, his belly distended from the treatment. He made the trip anyway.

Later, he managed to go through his books, making notes about who could benefit from one book or another after he was gone. The last time I talked to him was on the phone a few days before he died. I had called to find out how he was doing. We spent most of the short conversation talking about Hebrew grammar. Both my friends remained teachers until the last.

Much of my teaching career has been a search for a metaphor—an image that could successfully sum up what my colleagues and I do every day. In the past, I have suggested it is like dancing with our students. I have decided, however, that teaching is more like playing in a symphony. We practice individually every evening at home, but we play together every day at the university. We may play in separate rooms. But we are all, in some mysterious way, playing the same music.

I feel like a violinist who has been at his playing long enough to know a good musician when he hears one. We have lost two virtuosi. It is a bit like tuning my violin before an important performance and looking over to the oboe and flute sections to find two empty chairs. The orchestra will not be the same without them. There was a tenderness in both their playing which is not easy to find.

As I write, I glance out the window to discover a busy squirrel scampering up and down a cherry tree. The tree used to be nestled among a grove of elms. The elms are gone to disease.

Those elms will no longer bring a moment's beauty to the lives of sentient creatures. As I search for the vanished trees, I begin to understand the real tragedy of the deaths of my two friends. It is not just that her children are losing a loving mother, and their families a caring son and brother, a sister and devoted daughter. It is also that their music will be lost. There are generations of students who will be deprived of their art. We will refill their seats, but we cannot replace their music.

She was fifty-one years old. He was fifty-three. They should have played much longer.

An Adagio for Strings

In such a season, golden, spacious, but already whispering of the end, there will often come to a man a certain solemn mood, a vein of not unpleasing melancholy, and for a little while he will see all life moving to a grave measure, an adagio for strings.

J.B. Priestley
All About Ourselves and Other Essays

As I left the house one morning, a wedge of honking geese could be seen and heard making their way north. They were more like a boomerang of geese, really, for I know that after wintering in warmer climes most of them will return. In the fall, the sun once again begins its turning away from us. In a few weeks, the blush of leaves will be gone, as we settle in for what may prove to be a long winter. But the sun, too, eventually will return. It will make its wide arc, turning far, then near, until there is spring.

As a child at the beach on summer vacation, I used to think about the earth as a large hourglass. I thought God simply turned over the glass at the end of summer. The last grains of sand slipped through the narrow aperture, and we were sent back to school. The sand ran out again around Christmas time. Then, again, at Easter vacation. There was always enough time, then. When we ran out, God turned over the glass, making more time.

I married when I was thirty-nine years old. At our wedding my wife remarked about how many of my closest friends were people in the autumn of their lives. At the time I thought of her comment as little more than an off-hand observation. Since that time, many of these friends have suffered through serious illnesses, some have died. I now realize my wife watched her father go through a similar process of slowly losing older and wiser colleagues, so her wedding remark was born of tenderness and concern about what was to come. She knew I was already captivated by a senseless hope.

So now it is my turn. I watch so many of my closest friends retire from active teaching or writing. I watch their joints become stiff and painful, even though their minds are just as capable of earlier acrobatic feats. I wonder where the things they know will go? I wonder who will remember them after I am gone.

I no longer think of the world as an hourglass. If it is, all the sand seems to run one way. There is a poignancy and a melancholy about the autumn. It is not just the unspoken sharpness in the air. It is that the sharpness reminds me of departure, departure of these friends.

I sit at the keyboard composing lecture notes. I think if I immerse myself in the work, the fall, and a yearning for others' immortality, will go away. I look up for an instant and one drifting yellow leaf comes to a rest on the window sill. It is as pungent and melancholy as any hillside in New England. In the fall, days are not simply bright, but radiant, full of glory.

The fall, Keats' "season of mist and mellow fruitfulness," plays such cruel tricks on the human mind. It is as if autumn were the real creator, much more vibrant and spontaneous than spring. The colors are better, truer, more overwhelming. My older friends are so often the same way. It is as if it takes a good six or seven decades to get used to life, and then you begin to do some good work on the big questions. In one of his best letters, D.H. Lawrence suggests that one has to be seventy before one can get a firm grasp on the concept of courage. This is why so many of my friends are in their seventies and eighties.

It takes a certain kind of courage to be old; a variety more complicated than the momentary heroics of the battlefield.

I try to return to my lecture notes, but soon I look up again to find the leaf has vanished. If I had not seen it earlier, the leaf's existence, and now its disappearance, both would have gone unmarked. I wish the world were like an hourglass. Every year on the first day of fall, I carefully would turn it over one more time.

A Drone-Up Christmas

The Galilean has been too great for our small hearts.

H.G. Wells
Outline of History

My two-year-old son has begun calling his parents "drone-ups." The first time he said it, I thought it was a simple case of mispronunciation, but on this eve of Christmas, one of the most sacred days of the Christian calendar, I am beginning to wonder if the small boy is not already engaged in an important bit of parental character analysis, or perhaps a subtle kind of moral philosophizing.

Our adult lives—the ones we wish so fervently as children to inherit as soon as possible—do often drone on: monotonous, predictable, made of the same pragmatic stuff from day to day. This is one of the major reasons we need holidays, and holydays: to convince ourselves that our lives are not running down, unconnected to anything or anyone, like an eight-day clock left in a deserted house. We don't tell our children that this is the real purpose of Christmas—to break the monotony of self-interest in its many guises. We keep this secret from them until it is too late and they have tasted of the fruit of adulthood, and thus been duly banished from the garden.

My oldest son, an eight-year-old, has been eyeing the fruit of the tree of knowledge for most of this holiday season, but he has not yet decided to take a bite. He tells his parents he still believes in Santa Claus, searching our eyes for clues to something most of his classmates no longer see as a mystery. The older boy stills understands that Christmas requires his assent to the proposition that there exists a jolly stranger, a preposterous looking old man in a red suit and black go-go boots, who loves him almost as much as his parents do. And so, despite several discussions he has had with friends about the thermodynamics and space-time dimensions of portly men and narrow chimneys, and regardless of the clearly visible barcodes on all his toys, the boy appears safe from the ravages of adulthood for at least another year.

Most Christian adults enjoy Christmas because it is the only day of the year we can again act as children. On Christmas, charity flares up like a hot coal, but it burns out just as quickly. For too many adults, Christmas is made of equal parts of metaphysics and a peculiar variety of self-interest that, if not examined too closely, might pass for altruism.

Last month, homeless shelters and soup kitchens urged novice volunteers not to descend on them on Thanksgiving morning. It seems there is always a charitable log-jam on that day, as there is on Christmas morning. But most of us sleep-in the following morning, and everything goes back to normal, or at least as normal as it can be for those who live on the street. It is, of course, a curious fact about the English language that "alms" has no singular form. It is as if a singular act of charity a few days a year doesn't deserve the name.

Indian poet Rabindranath Tagore in *Stray Birds* suggests that the birth of every child brings with it the message that God is not yet fed up with the human race. It is a brilliant way for God to remind us what real charity is like: sending his only son. The purpose of children is to enlarge our hearts, to make us unselfish in ways we did not think possible. On Christmas, Christians are given a divine child, and in turn, this mysterious and defenseless infant gives our hearts a higher aim.

More than anything else, what Christmas does for Christian adults is that it reminds us, at least for the day, what Jesus meant Christianity to be: a resting place for the weary heart, a kind word for the wounded ear, a destination for unsure feet, and some good work to be finished by every hand.

The same God who is the foundation of hope, the object of love, and the subject of faith, sends us this small child every Christmas, and, at least for the day, it is hard to find a drone-up anywhere. It is a little known fact that it was not until the mid-fourth century that the Christian church decided, rather arbitrarily, to celebrate the birth of Jesus on December 25th. Judging by the ancient Patristic records, it could just as easily have been any other day of the year. Perhaps this is why Jesus appears to have approached every day as if it were Christmas. It's hard to act like a drone-up when you take his view.

On Advice

The advice of the elders to young men is very apt to be as unreal as a list of the hundred best books.

Oliver Wendell Holmes
Letters

The worst men often give the best advice.

P.J. Bailey
Letters

I was recently enlisted to do the prayer of the faithful at my niece's wedding. Tucked among the petitions for the poor and homeless, the needy and disenfranchised, was this: "For the ability to ignore almost all marital advice, no matter how freely and sincerely it is given, we pray to the Lord."

Now, just a few days later, before the wedding cake is even stale, it is difficult to describe the sheepishness with which I write this. I have been asked by the editor of *The Quill*, Mount St. Joseph's High School's student newspaper, to give you students some advice. I have been thinking that my only bit of counsel to you ought to be, "Don't listen to hypocrites." Perhaps the fact that I said "almost" in the petition gives me an out. I hope so.

Samuel Taylor Coleridge in a letter to a friend says that advice should be like snow: the softer it falls, the longer it dwells, and the deeper it sinks in. I'm not so sure he is right. In one of his best essays, Jonathan Swift suggests how difficult it is to give the young advice. He talks about how one can't give advice to those who won't even take heed of genuine warnings. When I was eighteen years old, I did quite a few dumb things. Back then, most of them were not lethal, now many of those dumb things are.

Perhaps this is the one bit of advice I can give you: don't do any dumb things. There, I've said it. It's not something that your parents have not already said to you about 150,000 times. I've had college friends die in automobile accidents. Almost always somebody was driving drunk. One of my favorite people from high school figured he would try LSD just one time. He dived out the dormitory window of a high-rise at Tulane University. At the time, he didn't realize how dumb it was.

People do dumb things for lots of reasons. When you are eighteen years old, it is often because other people are doing them too. Sometimes it is because we want desperately for certain people to like us, or because we are not quite sure who and what we are. You should know that it is sometimes dangerous to let other people decide who and what you will become. That's what happened to University of Maryland basketball star Len Bias, and my friend who dived out the window.

Doing dumb things often happens because no one in authority is watching you. There is an interesting irony in this fact. Most people wish to be respected for their character. If you wish to become the kind of person respected by others, there is a very simple formula: you need to learn how to do the good when no one else has an eye on you. If you can't do that, then you will forever be pretending to be and do the good. Others will know, even if you think you are very clever. Goodness so rarely consists simply in the outward things we do, but more often in the inward things we have become. You need to think of yourself as good before you can do the good.

One final thing: when I was eighteen years old, I thought money was very important. Now I don't. This is related to the last bit of advice I have for you. When a man is at the point of drowning, all he cares for is his life and for those he loves. But as soon as he gets ashore, he begins to worry that someone has stolen his towel.

The final piece of advice: don't worry so much about the towel. And good luck.

Chapter

Three

On Contemplation

Contemplation is the highest form of human life on condition that it be centered upon the object, the knowledge of which is the end of that life.

Etienne Gilson

All yearning, and thus all unhappiness, find their roots in time. We are most often unhappy when we wish the past to magically reappear, or when we desire the future to unfold before its time. The pieces in this third chapter are about the present. They are about those extraordinary moments: the catching of a firefly; the watching of snow fall; or swinging with a baby in the backyard hammock. In these moments yearning and desire disappear. In these times, a single moment can possess a kind of happiness that is eternal.

What Do Fireflies Think?

Here comes real stars to fill the upper skies,
and here on Earth come emulating flies.

Robert Frost
Fireflies in the Garden

This evening I am wondering about the consciousness of fireflies. My wife and five-year-old son have gone off to bed, and I sit alone on the back porch left to do the thinking. I can hear the bedsprings responding to their fitful sleep. In separate rooms, they turn this way and that, captured in a heat wave that envelopes the metropolis like an enormous plastic bag.

I mop my brow and search for a flashlight to read the ancient thermometer tacked to the frame of the back door: eighty-five degrees at midnight. Excessive heat has a way of instantly turning *homo sapiens* into thermal statisticians. The skinny wire coil attached to the screen door yawns, and I catch the door from popping my family awake. Then I remember them: the fireflies.

The heat must have hoodwinked them into believing that summer is half over—that the Orioles have made their climb from the cellar, that all the Desert Storm homecoming parades are finally over, that

Democrats and Republicans have come to some mutual understanding on a civil rights bill—and now it is time for the tiny bugs to make their mysterious yellow-green light.

The luminescent creatures first appeared in the high grass shortly after nightfall. By now they have risen to the full height of the ancient oaks that share the backyard with adolescent hemlocks and struggling wisteria. But this evening the yard is the property of the fireflies, and I am left to wonder what they are thinking.

Do they know they transform the night? Who turns their magic on and off and on again? Do they will the light, or is it simply a genetic accident? How long do they live and where do they go in daylight hours? What can the consciousness be like of these creatures whose brains are not much larger than the punctuation marks on this page? And yet they, unlike *homo sapiens*, seem to prefer sparking their own tail lights to cursing the collective darkness.

A few moments later I'm at the encyclopedia. I find "firefly" on page 791, between "firecrest" and "Firenze." But I find no satisfactory answer to why these small creatures have started tiny fires in my backyard.

Feeling my way back to the porch, I decide to count between the bugs' flashes of light. I quickly discover that there is no regularity to their illumination. It is haphazard, sporadic, the way time changes with the circumstances in which it is kept. I begin to speculate then that perhaps the firefly does measure time the way that humans do, but it is time measured by the heart. This is why they both so often glow.

Snow Ephemera

We sometimes wonder why the city government tilts so vigorously at the snow... Is snow such poisonous stuff? Our own feeling is that it is something to be honored and preserved.

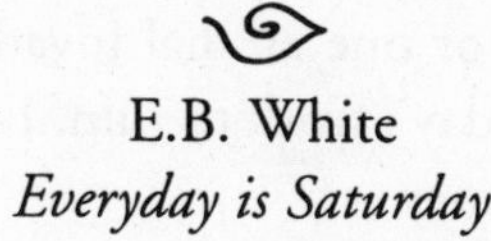

E.B. White
Everyday is Saturday

There is no real sense in trying unless you have genuine packing snow—the kind that falls as silently as dandruff—light, delicate flakes that drift to earth and lie together in a kind of fluffy mystical union. The snow must be slightly wet and clingy, not dry like the soap-powder snow spread on plywood Christmas gardens and crèches.

There are two basic techniques for making a snowman's round bottom layers. My wife is a packer—decisive, fast-acting, making it swiftly up as she goes. But I come from a long line of rollers—robust, patient types who begin with a fist-sized snowball. The rollers roll it this way and that, like the persistent dung-beetle and his scatological prize, until the snowball has grown to something Sisyphus might have proudly pushed uphill again and again and again.

This morning, while the snow is still fresh, my four-year-old son and I roll and shape, and roll some more. It is six weeks since Christmas, but the boy still has nutcrackers on his mind. After a few hours we are finished. Our sculpture looks like it has a thyroid problem. The boy makes a nutcracker hat out of construction paper, complete with a purple feather. There are no carrots to be found in the house, so the salvaged stem of a rotted pumpkin is placed between the black button eyes. As we step back to admire our creation, it looks like the Michelin Man in a sagging party hat, in bad need of a nose job. But to the boy, who knows well the story of *The Nutcracker*, it is Herr Drosselmeyer's gift to Clara.

While we roll and shape my mind drifts to other things. In activities such as these the mind is like a relay race, one idea rapidly passes the baton on to the next until, just a short time later, one discovers he has magically traveled great psychic distances.

One thought passed the baton this morning is that I have some sense now of what it must be like to be a spider, those strange, long-legged little creatures who spend their lives creating ephemera. One strong turn of the wind or one animal invading the high grass is all that is needed to bring a day's work to ruin. For a snowman artist, his creation is no less transitory.

As we roll and shape, I spend far more time watching the boy than I do watching our snowman. My son seems not to fret about the violence he witnesses on television, or even the inevitability of the thermometer on the back porch rising above thirty-two degrees.

All these thoughts hand the baton around for several minutes until I am given over to the idea of just how fitting it is that the color of snow—the stuff responsible for today's liberation from pre-school and the philosopher's study—is white, the color of innocence.

A moment later I begin thinking that innocence surely is more fragile than our snowman. It is perhaps the most sacred and the most fleeting of all ephemera. Innocence begins to desert them when snow becomes something balled into a weapon. It never returns.

When we have returned to the house and have snuggled up to read *The Nutcracker*, I begin thinking that there is a profound paradox in simplicity: that of all things, it is the most difficult to copy or to keep.

This thought causes me to wonder where my ability to live entirely in the moment has gone. And this thought passes the baton to a final musing, just as we are closing the book and getting ready for bed: I wonder why it does not snow more often.

The Borders of Sleep

I have come to the borders of sleep
The unfathomable deep
Forest where all must lose
Their way, however straight
They cannot choose.

Edward Thomas
Lights Out

Sleep is often the only occasion in which man cannot silence his conscience; but the tragedy of it is that when we do hear our conscience speak in sleep we cannot act, and that, when able to act, we forget what we knew in our dreams.

Erich Fromm
Man For Himself

I cannot remember when I began to suffer from insomnia. I suspect it came into my life with the same cunning as adulthood—no elaborate rite of passage, just a few more hairs on my chest and a different attitude toward the night.

As a child I was terrified of the dark; the sort who was always convinced that far more lay in wait beneath the bed than puffy gray dust balls my mother's housekeeping might have missed. Throughout childhood nights my parents kept a hall light burning, the door remained ajar enough to dispel the demons.

By adolescence, it became clear there really were monsters out there. They could be met on the street at night carrying handguns and sometimes wearing the most human of faces. In those years the hall light was extinguished in the late evening. Although sleep came more easily for me, it was more difficult for my parents who waited in the dark for my arrival home, the ash of my father's Chesterfield regular cigarette glowing in the dark of our living room.

In adulthood, the maturation process became complete. I began to learn that babies in prams are sometimes killed as part of "wars of liberation." It is coldly reminiscent of Dostoyevsky's speech delivered by Ivan Karamazov about the Turks—a macabre kind of nature imitating art. People are sometimes killed, not for who they are or for what they possess, but because they tragically symbolize something that must be destroyed. Often the victims don't know who has killed them, nor why they have died.

These days newspapers and television bring daily, indiscriminate death. It is called by many names: liberation, terrorism, retaliation, counter-insurgency, and low-intensity conflict. The effect is the same whatever we call it: people are dead and sleep is difficult.

In my sleep, the childhood monsters have returned. I seem to call them up in my dreams. Often I have seen their faces staring from national magazines. The images of killers and killed have been wedded together in a special kind of immortality. They remain alive in the depths of my unconsciousness until they are called forth in the dead of night. When this happens, I no longer remain in bed. I have learned to crawl from the covers to meet the night in a more rational way. A small night light now shines above my desk. It quickly allows me to get my bearings. Still, the night often hangs like a vapor. It begins just beyond the lamp and extends as far as my vivid imagination will take it.

This evening, I have been forced awake by a series of persistent images. Earlier in the day, while driving past the cemetery near my home, I stopped to look out over a field of flat copper grave markers, adorned with month-old holiday evergreens and bright red ribbons flapping in an unrelenting January wind. My grandfather lies sleeping beneath one of those markers.

This evening, in my sleep, the picture of that field has become wedded somehow to the recent images of bodies strewn in the disarray of death brought to two European airports ripped apart by terrorist bombs. The bodies of holiday travelers, lying in pools of blood, are marked A, B, C, and D.

In the middle of the night, I return to my desk. I am reminded of a poem by Josephine Jacobsen. In it she mentions certain inhabitants of Mexico who give names to the animals they are about to kill for food. Killing is terrible. Anonymous killing is unspeakable.

I begin to wonder what Christmas and Hanukkah, the Festival of Lights, will become for the families of these dead I did not know. I can feel a special kind of bitterness and resentment welling up in my chest. Strange, incomprehensible men traveling thousands of miles to murder absolute strangers.

The great bell atop the monastery near my home has just tolled four times—perhaps for A, B, C, and D. In a few hours, when the world has once again been knitted together from light to light, I will be angry with myself for feeling such hatred toward their murderers. But now, at the borders of sleep, in the dead of night, I do not.

The Heart's Desires

The central fire is desire, and all the powers of our being are given us to see, to fight for, and to win the object of our desire. Quench that fire and a man turns to ashes.

Basil Maturin
Laws of the Spiritual Life

For most of my life I have felt a craving for something. I'm not sure what. This unnamed desire, like the sultry voice of bachelorette number three on the old Dating Game show, hovers on the other side of the partition, communicative but disembodied. This secret desire—more like a longing, really—has remained so constant, so forceful, that I think of it as an inherent part of my life, something like a birthmark.

Before the longing entered me (I don't know how else to describe it), I used to think of myself as a sailor, bending over the maps of my possible lives, thinking of the many courses I might chart. But I no longer think of life that way. I now realize that the nature of the trip, including the destination, is determined far more by the wind and the tides than by any ideas the captain might have about where the craft is headed. The ancient Egyptians must have understood this. That is why the heart was the only organ they left intact in their mummies.

Over the past few years, living in the midst of a career, a growing family, and with a busy wife who wishes not to be considered the only caregiver at our house, I have come to understand that it is the desire, not the objects of desire, that has been so important to me along the way. The longing has had no simple referent; it is more like a condition than a destination. Meanwhile, the objects of the longing change daily. They compete with each other like a room full of children with a favorite teacher.

What has remained constant about my desires is that I so frequently seem to be under the spell of what is most distant, that it is the nature of my longings not to want what is near at hand. And so I tell my wife that I love her, and mean it most fervently, when she is away on an overnight business trip. When she is gone a few days, I walk into her closet and press her clothes to my face in order to experience the scent of her. When she returns, I do not let on, not because love is absent, but because the desire, the longing, somehow becomes replaced by another that demands more of my attention.

When I am away, I line up their pictures: my wife, our two small boys. I set them out on the hotel nightstand, next to the Gideon Bible—an assembly of talismans warding off the possibility of a life of loss. Before falling asleep, I try to remember every detail of their faces. Then I try to imagine a hole in the picture, like the old television commercials for life insurance. One by one I try to remove the faces until it all becomes too painful; however, I find the way to sleep, but the loss of my family usually follows me down into my dreams.

I know this sounds like a man with the right desires. Yet, when I return home a few days later, I get my wife to help with homework or to walk a fussy baby, because I have not finished reading the evening paper. Or I worry too much about the noise my seven-year-old makes, failing to realize that he makes the noise partly because he's happy and relieved to see me.

Too often when I am home, my life is taken up with an array of small things that go into the making of a big desire to be somewhere, anywhere else. I am perfectly willing to trade love and a sense of belonging, for thinner, more manageable desires: an uninterrupted cup of coffee, an hour to write, an evening of sleep unpunctuated by the sound of a baby crying. This willingness to trade desires goes on and on until eventually all that exists are the yearnings for the tiny things. The larger longings, mysteriously, seem to disappear for a time.

This is why I think of St. Valentine's Day as a special day, as important as Christmas or New Year's. It is a kind of secular Day of Atonement, when we publicly state the relative worthiness of our different desires. Some of my friends who, like me, are approaching middle age, have trouble sorting out the value of their longings. That is why they sometimes leave their wives and kids and buy new sports cars.

It isn't surprising that many of these men still send their ex-wives flowers on February 14th. Just for a moment, the relative importance of their desires becomes clear, as pristine as the first swipe of intermittent wipers. But then things get all cloudy again, and they need women half their age to fulfill new desires.

When St. Valentine's Day approaches, I always think about my longings as well, about how they are so frequently at odds with each other. I think that my relationship with those I love is like one of those Chinese finger locks I had as a child. The harder one pulls away, the tighter become the interlockings. I think about how love is a trap, but the quarry and the bait are identical. My friends who have left their families must have felt the same way, so they chew off their fingers like those desperate animals caught in steel traps in the woods.

What I like most about St. Valentine's Day are the cards and red boxes of candy—how the hearts are always laid open, lush and red, ready to be wounded or healed. The rest of the year our other desires conspire to make us clumsy surgeons busy with the knife, but for a single day in the coldest month of the year, we apply salve to the heart.

Blessed Golden Silence

All my days I have grown up among sages
and I have found nothing better for a person than silence.

Pirke Aboth
The Talmud

People go to take sun baths;
why have so few had the idea
of taking baths of silence?

Paul Claudel
Lord, Teach Us to Pray

Silence. It is a difficult thing to find these days. Susan Sontag, in a thoughtful book called *Styles of Radical Will*, suggests that the real art of our time consists primarily in making more noise than people in any age before us. Already in 1952, Max Picard in *The World of Silence* (the best book ever written about the subject) made the same point.

If you live anywhere close to what we call civilization, you know Sontag and Picard are surely correct. Jackhammers, boom boxes, the incessant whining of lawn mowers, motorists honking like demented geese, and beneath it all, at a much more pernicious level, it is the ubiquitous sound of television sets selling something just in earshot of those who, like the ancient ascetic Diogenes, roam the world (or perhaps just the house) for one example of real silence. John Cage sums up our present predicament in a book ironically called *Silence*: "There is no longer such a thing as silence. Something is always happening that makes a sound."

The omnipresence of noise, noise of almost infinite variety, is borne out by the language we use, or rather, that we choose no longer to use. When was the last time you heard the expression, "Silence is golden"? How about "Children should be seen and not heard"? Or "Mum's the word"?

The expression "the silence of the grave" is one that appears in ancient Hebrew, in classical Greek, and in all contemporary romance languages. But the spate of suggestions that we exhume Zachary Taylor, Abraham Lincoln, and William Casey have left me wondering if that turn of phrase is not long for this world, or the next one either.

In an old edition of the British *Who's Who*, writer Edith Sitwell once listed her hobbies as "reading, listening to music, and silence." Sitwell understood that silence, the real kind, is needed for people to be whole. Like air or water, it is a requirement for the soul's survival.

I am reminded of one reason why I enjoy the symphony. It is not simply the music. It is also the time between the movements, those small parcels of silence only sporadically interrupted by a cough or whisper. They are as valuable as the notes themselves. Indeed, the silence is the canvas on which the music is painted.

I have come to this understanding as I sit in the late afternoon on a deserted beach. The sun worshippers are gone. The blazing golden ball turns a fading pink as it dips below the wooden buildings at the dune line behind me. In its final act of the day, the sun casts long shadows on wet sand filled with the shells of dead horseshoe crabs.

Just beyond, the sea gathers itself in, and then rolls into a thundering crash. Today it is the gathering-in that has captivated me. For that brief moment, the great sea is silent. It is as if the ocean sighs before once again making the great roar.

I sit in those parcels of silence. In this small world without speech, I begin thinking that silence is one of those remaining phenomena that have yet to be noisily exploited, for clearly silence is seen by most people as useless.

A moment later, in the next silence, I begin to understand that it must have been this way before creation. This exercise gives new meaning to twentieth-century philosopher Ludwig Wittgenstein's aphorism that the real wonder is that there is something rather than nothing.

Why would God create? It must have been terribly painful tearing open the silence.

Swinging

Thou foster-child of silence, and slow Time.

John Keats
Ode on a Grecian Urn

We are in the midst of the dog days, so sticky and absent of promise. In the morning, mist rises from a soaked lawn, dissolving into oppressive afternoons bent on turning us all into watchers of the heat index. It's ninety-seven degrees, but according to the heat index it feels like 114. "It's not the heat, it's the humidity," leaps off the tongues of all those who have not escaped to the mountains or the beaches.

The knot of summer days unties itself invisibly like a thief, and I am left swinging with a baby in a hammock, a present from the boy and his older brother on Father's Day. For a teacher there is little to do in these days—a steamy netherworld somewhere between the spring term's final exams and the first blush of September's new students. And so, to avoid the heat, and perhaps to recover something lost, we swing.

In this dog-day swinging, the boy and his father have found a land of silence, a place where surface is the essence. No stripping down is needed, no insistent teacher-student questions about what is absolutely here. Just the silent understanding between us that there is love, and a certain stillness, in the swinging.

In winter so much is closed and hidden. The landscape stands bleak and static. It is best for us to stay inside, even if it means moving about in an atmosphere of claustrophobia and noise. In winter, at least for the father, the discerning eye so often is left to find its way in an inward night.

But here, in the heat—and in the hammock—I am nourished as by sound sleep after deep pain. The smallest of my veins drinks slow-time and I can breathe again. In summer, time beats as truly as our hearts, but it beats by a slower rhythm. Its pendulum swings silently, languidly, like a small boy and his father in a hammock full of happiness.

We swing and silently rejoice in the outward forms of summer's light: a sparrow hopping from branch to branch; the ancient shadow of an old shed splaying its dark geometry across a green field; the sun and trees repositioning themselves with every tilt of the head, every swing of the hammock. The green seems a mysterious liquid that moves from one tree to the next, like tender words passed between lovers in the making of a child.

After a few moments, I can feel the boy's breathing synchronize with mine. Our chests rise and fall together, our hearts slow together, we swing...and swing...and swing. In my mind the motion and the smell of the boy become silently, eternally married to summer.

Someday, this boy will learn that we live here between two great silences—the silence of the not-yet and the silence of the grave. If he is like his father, he will try to make sense of these silences, so full of nothing. But the silence of the here and now, the silence amidst the lattice-work of this rope hammock is of a different kind, for it is made of something. In this silence the boy seems to understand as well as his father that sometimes for hearts to be filled to the brim they must first be made still.

For so much of my life, I have understood how often the heart forces us to speak, sometimes more to wound than to heal. But today, in the hammock, perhaps for the first time, it insists on this new silence...and the stillness...and the swinging.

Cor ad Cor

There is an awful warmth about my heart
like a load of immortality.

John Keats
Letters

Controlling one's heart is as easy as cutting
granite with a razor, or mooring a ship with
a single silken thread.

John Henry Newman
Letters

I remember my mother hanging clothes in winter light. It was St. Valentine's Day, and tiny icicles had formed on the wooden clothes pins that held my father's stiff work shirts to the frozen line. I stayed home sick from school, though the evening before I methodically had prepared the small red hearts I planned to distribute to a few favorite girls among my sixth grade classmates. But Eros does not always hit his mark, and, with the help of some fortuitous microbes, I spent the day with my mother—a day filled with the smells of hot chocolate and a baking cake.

I remember sitting in the kitchen staring out at the frozen wash hanging on the line. I remember thinking how appropriate it is that St. Valentine's Day, the feast of warm hearts, comes in the coldest month of the year. By February, winter has come in earnest, revealing the skeleton of things. Sparrows put on plain brown overcoats. We are all in great need of warmth, the way a walk in the basement requires light.

The soul experiences winter as much as the body. The falling temperatures only make it worse. A winter in the soul too often dwells on the monotony in affection. It sometimes leads to an indifference in the expression of kindness toward those with whom we are most intimate. Love should open the heart like a rose. In the soul's winter, it closes it like a cabbage. This is why we have St. Valentine's Day: to remind us that the heart has many hiding places. It also has doors. In winter too many of them are bolted shut. St. Valentine's Day reminds us to keep at least one door ajar. The right person may happen along, or maybe a thief. St. Valentine's Day convinces us that, either way, it is worth taking the chance.

Isadora Duncan called the heart a pastime and a tragedy. Flaubert spoke of the heart as a cemetery: we carry the departed around in our hearts. But the dearly departed include more than the dead. The heart also contains those former loves we have tried to ignore, but never quite manage to forget. These lost loves live secretly in some of the heart's locked rooms. Sometimes, like a persistent burglar, they manage to pick these locks in our dreams.

Lost loves are an important part of the economy of the heart, unless the heart makes a stone of itself. Lost loves must find their place, or the beating of the heart begins to sound too much like an empty steel drum, or a dried nut rattling around in its dusty shell.

In the heart there is always a kind of order, a regularity of inner forces, binding the possessors by different ties to different loves, living and dead, found and lost. These ties all have their consequences; the most important one is that they make us the people we have become.

When I memorized a cherished poem as a child, my maternal

grandmother called the process "learning by heart." It is neither the brain nor the mind that remembers certain things. It is the heart. And it is the heart that traces every line of my wife's face when she is away. It is the heart that regularly allows her to display a curious kind of active imagination when it comes to my virtues. This is because the heart is a gentle, tender prison. To avoid solitary confinement, love magnifies both its object and its subject.

Blaise Pascal suggests in his *Pensées* that sometimes the heart has reasons that the mind will never know. That is why it is the heart alone that understands what is perhaps the greatest of love's many paradoxes: when the heart is empty, it soon becomes too small to be inhabited by even the most ardent of visitors. But when the heart is crowded, it always manages to find more room.

Wonder

Misshapen, black, unlovely to the sight,
O mute companion of the murky mole,
You must feel overjoyed to have a white
Imperious, dainty lily for a soul.

Richard Kendrell Munkittrick
A Bulb

The person who cannot wonder, who does not habitually wonder...is like a pair of spectacles, behind which there sits a pair of blind eyes.

Thomas Carlyle
Sartor Resartus

I used to believe that the loss of wonder was merely a symptom of our age. In my job I spend a good bit of time living in the ancient world. The ancients have always seemed to me more capable of letting the miraculous be, and thus they were more able to be amazed. This is why Socrates thought that philosophy, the love of wisdom, began in wonder, and Aristotle in his *Rhetoric* suggested that wonder, more than any other human ability, implies an intense desire to learn. Above all else, Socrates and Aristotle were always looking for a good surprise.

Livy, an ancient Roman historian, tells us in his *History* that the Romans had a nine day festival devoted to the human propensity for amazement. But already in the first century we find Roman poet Lucretius lamenting in his *De Rerum Natura* the fact that "nothing is so great nor so wonderful that we don't all, little by little, begin to lose our capacity to wonder."

If Lucretius is correct, then the loss of wonder comes not with technological advancement, but with the arrival of adulthood. As children, we all had this priceless talent for amazement, but as time slips into that invisible place where hope loses its feathers, we get too used to life and wonder disappears. We become like people who live next to the Grand Canyon but never think to look down.

Perhaps this is one of the unexamined reasons for having children. They constantly remind us of what it was like when we were most fully alive. My two-year-old son is amazed by the water that comes from the spigot. He easily becomes engrossed in the anatomy of an earthworm, in the day's arching journey of the sun, or in the movement of his shadow. Compared to him, I am merely a part-time wonderer for I, too, often succumb to the habitual. The boy knows nothing of habit. This is why he has a much better understanding than his father of the importance of pleasure in itself.

My son reminds me that April is not the cruelest month, it is the most wondrous one. Everything is blooming recklessly. In spring, the colors are like voices, and the yard becomes a chorus with each voice singing beautifully in its own language. The little boy seems to hear these voices. He sees the beauty of each flower without naming it, without knowing its fate. I know many of the botanical names, but I do not see flowers the way he does. Watching him in the yard, among the flowers, it becomes clear to me, as if for the first time, that wonder is the qualitative distance God places between human beings and himself, for it is wonder that most keenly requires us to find the truth.

It is only in fatherhood, and in the writing life, that I ever achieve any lasting sense of wonder. I imagine this is the difference between myself and real writers. The real writer lives in a permanent state of amazement. Beneath all the other transitory feelings about economics, politics, or religion there always lies a deep vein of astonishment. All good writing is simply an attempt at conveying that amazement. All good writing is little more than taking on the wonderment of a child and realizing that play is more fundamental than work. All good writing is a matter of taking on the wonderment and finding a way to keep it until finally the game is called because of darkness.

Jerry's House of Ideas: New and Used

The very nature of philosophy is speculative. It must be ever on the hunt.

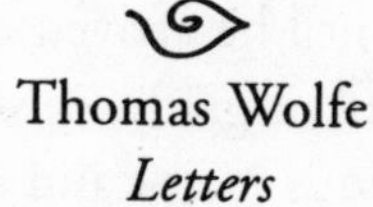

Thomas Wolfe
Letters

Professor S.V. Sisyphus has finished frantically searching through the last of his desk drawers. He sat back uneasily in his swivel chair and stared above his desk at the picture of that ancient Greek orator Demosthenes talking about philosophy with marbles in his mouth. There was really no getting around it. A new semester was about to begin and the good professor had run out of philosophical insights. He had looked through his office. He had searched his book-lined study at home. The result was the same: Sisyphus was tapped out of trenchant philosophical reflections, just as his fall classes were about to resume.

He made a quick trip to the campus bookstore, then he hurried to the library, but he came up dry in both places. When he inquired of the reference librarian when she might be expecting some fresh philosophical insights, she just looked over her bifocals and whispered, "There is no way of telling, you know how these things are."

When he finally arrived at Philosophers' Mall, it was with a great deal of apprehension, even what Heidegger might call "angst." It all looked so big and impressive. He could not get over how much Philosophers' Mall had grown since he last saw it. One thing he did know for certain: this was his last chance.

Professor Sisyphus walked to the fountain at the center of the mall. It was there that he found the *Existentialists' Directory*, a large box-shaped illuminated structure of multi-colored plastic and wood. On its flat surface was a detailed map of the mall fashioned by a nihilist. It included a large red movable arrow on which was printed: YOU ARE NOT HERE.

He felt a dizzying nausea, and began to wander aimlessly past the posters of Kierkegaard and William of Ockham displayed in the window of the Idea Outlet, past the children's' store, Plato'n'Things, past the large blue and white sign announcing the arrival next month of the Solipcist convention, until he arrived at the Syllogism Barn.

The place was packed full of graduate students bickering over who had legitimate claim to various major and minor premises strewn atop a sale counter. One small, bespeckled man refused to relinquish a conclusion he held tightly in his fist. A much larger man, a phenomenologist, held just as tightly to the two premises to which the conclusion led.

Professor Sisyphus picked through the bin marked: "Realizations, 25% off." He found a *cogito ergo sum* and a spare *esse est percipe* or two, but there was nothing fresh to be found there. He stared vacantly for a while at the display case full of conundrums and paradoxes. A few mathematicians crowded him away from the case, but there was really nothing there he could use.

Finally, the professor wandered over to the large department store at the end of the mall. The full weight of his predicament was now beginning to take hold. In less than twenty-four hours he would be back in class, with nothing of real philosophical importance to say. When he stepped off the elevator, the Notions Department was full of the usual inclinations and beliefs, but nothing of the innovative and clear substance Sisyphus was seeking. He checked through the bins marked reflections, cogitations, and lucubrations; he looked through the sale displays full of speculations, ponderings, and ruminations; but nothing caught his philosophical fancy.

As despondent as a pessimistic Schopenhauerian whose gone off his Prozac, Sisyphus walked absent-mindedly back through the center of the mall until he felt moved, as if guided by some unknown Mall Manager, to Jerry's House of Ideas: New and Used. It was a small shop undergoing some major deconstruction, but it was in the back where he found the pristine insight for which he had been searching. It had been thrown into a bin marked "Reconsiderations, Second Thoughts, and Retrospectives: All Sales Final."

It was a line from Socrates: "The wise man is the man who knows he knows nothing."

"And it's in the public domain," the philosopher whispered.

He would use it.

Chapter

Four

On *Homo Ludens*

It is the heart that is not yet sure of its God that is afraid to laugh in His presence.

George MacDonald

I have found that the most difficult pieces to write are often the humorous ones. *Homo ludens* (man at play or man the laugher), at least in my life, is often in great danger of extinction. I am by most peoples' accounts a serious man. Still, there is much to find funny, if not absurd, in much of what I and those around me say and do. I have tried to capture some of those examples of *homo ludens* here in this chapter. I have included in this chapter a few short pieces on baseball, the most perfect of human games.

Ticket Metamorphosis

Kafkaesque: referring to Franz Kafka;
a bizarre or hopeless situation.

Webster's New Collegiate Dictionary

Gregor Samsa awoke one morning to discover he had not received his opening day Oriole tickets. It was no dream.

Gregor managed to fix his six pairs of spindly legs in his specially made orange and black double-knit slacks and headed for the light rail. As he swung his VW Beetle into the Timonium park-and-ride, he discovered that the eighty places had been taken by automobiles with stickers from the Ruxton-Riderwood Community Association, so he couldn't take the light rail.

Before Gregor left the house he had called the Oriole offices. The lady on the other end of the line told him he must have lost the tickets. She said they were scheduled to be mailed out last week. She said that there was a possibility that Gregor's mail had been tampered with. She said that the Orioles had gone to great trouble and that Gregor should be thankful that he lived in a free country where we had an opportunity to make the special opening day tickets that never came.

Gregor headed toward the stadium by way of the Jones Falls Expressway. A few moments later, the expressway became a parking lot. Several thousand other people had had their mail tampered with, and they were headed to the stadium to wait in line for their opening day tickets. Thousands of cars waited on the expressway, so that soon they could wait in line at the ticket window. They all felt guilty.

When Gregor finally pulled his car off the expressway, he discovered the Orioles had scheduled a parade at the same time, so that it would be particularly difficult to find a place to park. He found a space in Little Italy. He traveled as fast as his little legs would carry him. When he finally arrived at the ticket line, he waited for twenty minutes until one of the nice ushers with the new uniforms informed him that he had been standing in line with people who were waiting to pay $3 so they could watch the Orioles have batting practice on an off day. Gregor felt very guilty.

When Gregor finally found the proper line, he waited for thirty-five minutes until he got his turn at the window. He tried to be polite. He knew what repercussions there can be when one is not. While he was waiting his turn Larry Luchino, president of the Orioles organization, went by in the parade. Gregor waved four of his arms.

At first, the man at the ticket window insisted that there was absolutely no record that anyone named Gregor Samsa had ever existed. Gregor pushed his driver's license through the window opening. They argued a while longer, Gregor's feelers standing upright in excitement and indignation.

Finally, the man at the ticket window told Gregor that he must have lost the tickets. Gregor insisted that he hadn't. The man suggested Gregor's mail must have been tampered with. The man finally gave Gregor new tickets, but he never explained how there could have been two sets of tickets for the same seats the same day, if one set had already been mailed out. The man kept Gregor's driver's license, just in case the authorities needed to get in touch with him later. Gregor felt very guilty.

On the way home, Gregor thought about how the Orioles had promised him tickets "comparable" to those he had in the old stadium. He wondered whether the authorities had something to do with his new seat assignment, which seemed much farther away than his old seats. Gregor mused about how he and the other citizens of the state had paid for the new stadium. He knew how strange the world could be, but he wondered why no one had said "thank you." Gregor thought about all this a while longer. All of this made him feel very, very guilty.

On the way home, Gregor was stopped by the police for speeding. He didn't have his driver's license with him. It was no dream.

Accu-Wife

We regret to inform you we are unable to bring you the weather report from the airport, which is closed because of the weather. Whether we are able to bring you the weather tomorrow depends on the weather.

Arab News, quoted by Stephen Pile,
in *The Book of Heroic Failures*

My wife worships at the Temple of the Five-Day Forecast. Willard Scott is her bishop, Bob Turk her local priest and prophet. She greets reports from the National Weather Service with the deference devout Catholics accord to papal encyclicals.

My spouse rises early every morning, quickly drinks her coffee, and turns her attention to the weather map in the morning paper.

"Oh, it's going to rain on Friday," she says on Monday morning, as she glumly scans the five-day "Accu-Weather" forecast. She makes this prediction gravely, with the same zeal and surety I imagine John Calvin had when he mounted the steps of his sixteenth-century Geneva pulpit to tell his followers that God had already consigned most of them to eternal damnation.

By the time Friday rolls around, there's hardly a cloud in the sky, but my wife is far too worried about the following Wednesday's forecast to notice that Accu-Weather was not so accurate after all.

With the weather we've been having in Baltimore this summer, my wife's morning pronouncements have taken on a more urgent character. They have acquired the air of an apocalyptic visionary anxiously studying the book of Revelation to decide whether to invest in another five-day deodorant pad.

Over the past several months, my wife has become a kind of barometric Nostradamus. On Tuesday morning she wanders around the house muttering to herself, "High in the low 90s for church on Sunday . . . I guess we should still go . . . what do you think?"

Recently, I have begun keeping score on how well the folks at "Accu-Weather" are doing. They are right only about half of the time. When I pointed out this fact to my wife, however, she displayed all the skepticism of those retirees who sent their Social Security checks to Oral Roberts a few summers ago so God would not "take him home."

"Yes, honey" she replied earnestly, "but there's a 40 percent chance of rain next Thursday for Owen's Little League practice."

I can't help thinking there is a kind of hubris in all this that I just can't muster. Perhaps it has something to do with my skepticism about the sign that stood outside my Catholic grade school for decades: "Bingo Thursday Night." I used to worry that maybe that sign was tempting fate just a little too much. I could imagine God on his lofty throne looking down at the sign and proclaiming, "Oh, yeah, well we'll just see about that."

But my wife brings me back from my mystical reverie: "Do you think we should cancel the July 4th picnic?" she inquires on June 30th. "It's supposed to rain."

Not satisfied with the degree of prescience offered by the five-day forecast, she came home from work one evening with a *Farmer's Almanac* tucked under her arm. She has been looking for new ways to extend her vision of world weather patterns into the future.

"The heat's going to last clear into October," she said gravely, glancing up from the almanac.

"No kidding," I reply, catching the spirit of the moment. "I think we'd better cancel Halloween."

Disney-Whirl: Some Mickey Machinations

It is a dreadful thing, sir,
To awaken again an old will that lies quiet.
Yet still I long to know.

Sophocles
Oedipus at Colonus

I love Mickey Mouse more than any woman I have ever known.

Walt Disney
Interview, *Life*, 1958

When Donald Duck celebrated his sixtieth birthday, he didn't get the attention Mickey Mouse did a few years prior when he had his fiftieth. The ducks birthday reminded me that I never really liked Mickey or Donald. I just couldn't get into the whole *Weltanschauung*, as nineteenth-century German philosophers and some of my graduate students with a keen "world view" would say.

I am usually able to repress my feelings about Donald and Mickey.

This ability makes my life more manageable. But the announcement of the birthday awoke in me a whole series of misgivings about these animated animals that I have been harboring—buried, but apparently not forgotten—since early childhood.

It is still not clear whether my early interests in mysteries, great and small, predisposed me to these unnecessary worries about Mickey and Donald, or if the brooding about the cartoon pair laid the dangerous groundwork for a perilous and thus fabulously lucrative life in philosophy. Whatever the truth may be, it was clear to me, from a very early age, that the stories of Mickey, Donald, and their closest friends and relations were fraught with an impressive series of philosophical and conceptual problems—puzzles, wide and deep.

I have remained silent about these worries for too long. But in the interest of inter-species relations, plain decency, and what Richard Nixon once labeled "full disclosure," I feel compelled to speak out.

Perhaps my most vexing worry about the Disney duo is why Mickey wears red trousers with suspenders, while no one wears pants in the Duck family. Donald, his uncle Scrooge McDuck, and the nephews all go bottomless. This seems to be a "genetic thing," as George Bush might say. Nevertheless, Senators Strom Thurman and Jessie Helms have yet to speak out about the matter.

While we are on the question of animal nudity, why does Mickey have a canine friend (Goofy) who walks upright, wears overalls, and speaks English, and a pet (Pluto) who barks like your basic dog, wears only a flea collar, and happily walks on all fours? Why don't Goofy and Pluto spend more time together? I should think they would have a lot in common. And why does the smart one live in the dog house?

Why does Donald speak with an accent, while Mickey and Minnie do not? And why doesn't Minnie have a pair of sensible shoes? Other than June Cleaver and a few ostentatious cross-dressers, no one but Minnie wears pearls and stiletto heels to a picnic. And what exactly is the nature of the relationship between Mickey and Minnie? They live in separate houses, but they have the same last name.

Are both Mickey and Donald estranged from their siblings? Both have nephews (how do you tell Huey and Dewey apart?), but there is never any mention of their having brothers or sisters.

Does Minnie only have one pair of underwear (the frilly white and red polka-dot ones), or do all the undies she owns look exactly the same? And why is she still letting people see her underwear at her age? This, of course, leads quite naturally to an even more vexing question: why do we call it a *pair* of underwear?

These are puzzles, wide and deep. I hope I am not around for Donald's seventieth birthday.

A Field of Phantoms

It is all right for the beasts to have no memories; but poor humans have to be compensated.

William Bolitho
Camera Obscura

Today I begin a process of anticipatory grief. The actual death will come later this year, September 6, 1991, to be exact. On that day, if all goes well, the Baltimore Orioles will retire the Detroit Tigers in the top of the ninth inning, and the lights will be turned off at Memorial Stadium for the final time. For a while longer, the infield grass will continue to grow, like the fingernails and hair of the dead. But a short time later, the building will change its ontological status: a wrecking ball will magically relegate concrete and steel to the province of memory, the only paradise from which we are never fully evicted.

I know when September 6th comes I will be reminded of the disconnecting of the respirator of a supposedly terminal patient. We will watch the building breathe its last, but debate will continue long afterwards about whether the patient on 33rd Street should have been declared beyond help.

The arguments for and against the new stadium, in the face of the destruction of the old one, almost seem irrelevant. The discussions remind me of the end of the biblical book of Job. In the final chapter of the book, God gives Job a new set of ten children to replace those who were taken from him in the beginning of the tale. These children are clearly better than the old set, by any objective measure.

But the authors of the biblical book tell us nothing about whether the patriarch from Uz yearned for the dead children, despite the beauty and intelligence of the new kids. The biblical writers leave us in the dark about Job's memories of the first set of kids. They don't tell us if the ghosts of the old children continue to haunt the middle of their father's head. Vladimir Nabokov, in a very powerful essay on the nature and uses of memory, suggests that the more one loves a memory, the stronger and stranger the memory becomes. Certainly he is correct about those who have vanished from our lives, whether they be people or buildings.

Memorial Stadium houses phantoms. I go there a few dozen times a summer to watch baseball games, but I also go to commune with those spirits. My father took me to see Willie Miranda go deep in the hole to get Mickey Mantle by half a step. I am reminded of that play every time I go there. There is the image of Mike Devereaux hitting the leftfield foul pole, and Jimmy Orr stretching out like Nureyev in the corner of the end zone. As Proust suggests, "Time changes people, but it does not alter the memory of them."

It matters little that the new stadium will be a better one. One ought not to boast about his second wife when the first has just met an untimely death. We might readily admit that Memorial Stadium was the kind of building an architect friend of mine had in mind when he said, "It has all the earmarks of an eye sore." But we must recall that buildings express the character and the needs of their age. The 1950s were a simpler, more broad-shouldered age, a time for unironed steel and concrete. It was an age without the need for skyboxes.

Perhaps the old stadium is too simple a building for too complex an age. But what are we to do with the phantoms? Are we to evict them? Where will they stay? Or will they wander aimlessly in the underworld, like a Greek tragedy? And what are we to do with our simpler selves? And what are we to do with the phantoms?

Ernest Dimmet once remarked, "Architecture, of all the arts, is the one that acts the most slowly but the most surely on the soul." Dimmet was surely right—particularly when a building housing forty years of phantoms becomes a ghost itself.

The Return of the Mundane Mysteries

Mysteries are not necessarily miracles.

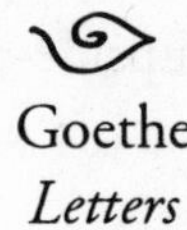

Goethe
Letters

Several summers ago I published an article about how I get paid to think all year long (from September to June, that is) about some of life's more perplexing and intractable conundrums: Does God exist? Is there an answer to the problem of innocent suffering? Are there objective standards for the moral good, or is ethics simply a subjective matter? Through fall, winter, and spring, I receive a check every two weeks for thinking about things that keep others awake in the middle of the night. With the first signs of summer, however, my mind turns to smaller metaphysical matters, what rightfully might be called "Mundane Mysteries."

For years I have kept a file on these petit perplexities. Every now and then I publish another batch, usually about the time the snowball stand opens and the sun begins to soften the tar on the road. I come forth with these in the sincere wish that someone out there may have some answers. Please do not send more mundane mysteries. I have all I can comfortably handle.

And so, without further ado, here are ten of my favorites:

- What does "without further ado" mean?

- Why is it never the heat but always the humidity?

- What is it with Jerry Lewis and the French? I just don't get it. Am I missing something about Jerry Lewis that the average sophisticated French person clearly sees?

- How come no clairvoyants ever win the lottery? Why don't we see more fortune tellers at the track or working on the stock change?

- Why hasn't Dick Butkus changed his name by now?

- Why is the opposite of upside-down, rightside-up? Shouldn't it be upside-up?

- Why do speakers use the expression "each and every one?" What does the "every" part add that the "each" part or the "one" part didn't already give you? This is the only triple redundancy regularly used in the English language.

- Why is it that when a human being goes crazy we say he cracked up or had a breakdown?

- Why is it that when a car cracks up that means it hit another car, but when it breaks down it means that it doesn't work properly anymore?

- How does anybody ever learn English as a second language?

And here's an extra, absolutely free:

- If you built a space ship and traveled to Saturn at the speed of light, what would happen if you turned your headlights on?

Requiem for a Stadium

Some memories are realities, and are better than anything that can ever happen again.

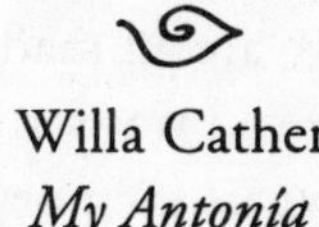

Willa Cather
My Antonía

I was there the day Memorial Stadium died. If you were not, I know you probably wanted to be. You are like distant relatives who could not make the trip, and the funeral home only held so many mourners.

I want to tell you about it. I want to tell you about how thousands of grown people cried. They cried when retiring pitcher Mike Flanagan was brought on to strike out the only two batters he faced in the top of the ninth.

They cried when Cal Ripken hit into a double play to make the last of the last outs. They cried not because he grounded out, but because he was Cal Ripken, the only remaining link to an era when ballplayers were good and Memorial Stadium was good enough.

We thought about the stadium then as Memorial Stadium. We thought it would last forever, even if we, creatures who succumb to time and tragedy, do not. We listed the names of our war dead on the wall and in our hearts, hoping that the brick and mortar would out live us. It did not.

The real tears came that final day after the last out was made. They began when Brooks Robinson stepped out on the field to take up his familiar station at the hot corner. He was followed by Frank Robinson and then Jim Palmer and all the others. Rick Dempsey, that scrappy catcher, came. Feisty long-time manager Earl Weaver kicked dirt on a hole that used to be home plate.

Old men, wearing familiar numbers, trotted to their former positions, many limping with an unfamiliar gait. This was when the real tears came. They came with the realization that the field—that dazzling garden of green and tan—had not aged a day since 1954. There was that strange juxtaposition that come only at the best of wakes: the marriage of the infinite and the finite, the spiritual and the corporeal. These were old men, eternally young in the mind's eye, who had returned to remind us that we are all made of protoplasm and hope.

It was a beautiful day. The sun was setting when we left. And God was reminding us why he gave us memory.

The Season of the Asterisk

All winter long I am one for whom the bell is tolling;
I can arouse no interest in basketball,
indoor fly-casting , or bowling;
The sports pages are strictly no soap,
And until the cry Play Ball! I simply mope.

Ogden Nash
Sports Illustrated
April 15, 1957

Perhaps only one thing was clear: they would no longer call Roger Maris's brush with immortality the season of the asterisk. The strike-riddled 1995 major league baseball season had been one for the record books. Beginning in spring training with the block buster trade that sent the entire Baltimore Orioles team to Tampa Bay for the Buccaneers, it had seemed more like a season authored by Franz Kafka than by the baseball gods. Peter Angelos, pressed to field a team by the new baseball commissioner Marge Schott, swapped Malcolm Glazer for the Bucs even-up, thus avoiding the use of baseball scabs, while bringing NFL football back to Baltimore.

Joel Glazer, the new general manager and director of player personnel for the Orioles, within hours of the trade, called a news conference to announce that after almost twenty years of unsuccessful attempts to fill Brooks Robinson's shoes at third base, the Orioles finally had signed someone to do the job: Brooks Robinson.

But despite this and other front office moves, the Orioles came limping out of the gate. By September, however, they were coming down the stretch neck and neck with the Red Sox. The Birds ended the regular season sweeping the Toronto Blue Jays who finished in third, with a record of eighty-one and eighty-one, having played all 162 games on the road. The Bosox faded in the final week of the season, however, losing three of four to the Indians at home.

Sherman "Babe" Obando, the Orioles right-fielder, by the last day of September had hit his sixty-second home run on a high fastball offered up by Syd Finch, a rookie southpaw for the Chicago White Sox. The White Sox had won the Western Division title in the American League, chiefly on the strength of the arms of Oil Can Boyd and Steve Carlton, the legs of their rookie center-fielder, Michael Jordan, and the bat of their veteran designated hitter, Minnie Minoso. But the Oriole rotation of Jim Palmer, Charley Hough, Hoyt Wilhelm, and nineteen-year-old left-handed flame-thrower Hirohito Suzuki, won the American League championship series in four straight games.

Over in the National League it was just as strange a year. Glenn Davis hit twenty-seven home runs in spring training, only to miss the entire regular season due to being hit by lightning when he carried the lineup card to home plate on a rain-delayed opening day. The Niekro brothers, Phil and Joe, pitched the Atlanta Braves to within one game of the Eastern Division title, but the Braves' entire 106-win season was forfeited when it was discovered that Pedro Dellarosa, Atlanta's mustachioed first baseman, was really Pete Rose. Later, it was revealed that during the All-Star game's home run derby Rose had made a bet with Indians first baseman Albert Belle that he would not be detected the entire season, and double or nothing on winning the National League batting championship.

The real story of the 1995 season, however, came down to the final day. The Dodgers' Bert Blylevan, the first pitcher to win thirty games in nearly three decades, all season long provided a steady diet of curve balls that the National Leaguers found hard to hit. Blylevan already had pitched games one and four of the series, beating Palmer on a four hitter, and losing to Hoyt Wilhelm, when pinch hitter Floyd "Sugar Bear" Rayford hit the left field flag pole in the top of the ninth at Dodger Stadium.

Game seven saw the Dodgers go ahead 2–1 on a suicide squeeze. Bill Lee had started for the Dodgers, giving up one run on five hits through four innings, but Lee developed a blister in the top of the fifth, and he was followed by Mark "The Bird" Fidrych who lasted two, and then Tommy John who pitched a scoreless eighth.

Obando came to bat in the top of the ninth. Cesar Devarez had walked to start the Oriole half of the inning. After pinch hitter Jim Traber (who had sung the national anthem before the game) struck out on ball four, and Harry Berrios popped to the catcher while trying to bunt the runner over, Devarez stole second. This set the stage for Obando who had won games two and three on home runs.

Ken Dixon and Joachim Andujar had been warming for Los Angeles for most of the eighth, but after a short trip to see Tommy John, Dodger manager Tommy Lasorda yanked him and brought back the ancient curve-baller, Blylevan.

With a 3-2 count, Obando went deep, but a foot foul. Everyone on earth knew what the next pitch would be. It looked like it rolled off a table-top. Obando wobbled at the knees, taking strike three.

Marge Schott had trained her dog to carry the World Series trophy in his jaws. She stood on the makeshift stage in the Dodger locker room with the dog and manager Lasorda who earlier had said he would use scab players only after the dead come back to life. A dusty Walter O'Malley accepted the trophy from Marge. Then things went a little crazy in the Dodger locker room.

Meanwhile, on the other coast, George Steinbrenner was busy hatching a plan to assure that the 1996 baseball season would be an even more exciting one for the fans. Already he had managed to contact all but a few scrubs from the newly resurrected 1927 New York

Yankees. Their skills were a little rusty, but all but the Babe said they were willing to play for their 1927 salaries. Rumor has it that he is going to ask oft-hired, now deceased manager Billy Martin back one more time. "Death and baseball," George said to himself with a wry smile, "an unbeatable combination."

Rumors continued to fly about the Yankee owner's plans. Some of the other owners were a little upset when they heard that Steinbrenner was thinking of using dead people as substitute players. When contacted at his home, Mr. Steinbrenner was quoted as saying, "What's the big deal? If we let dead people vote, why shouldn't we let them play baseball?"

On Foolishness

Hain't we got all the fools in town on our side?
And hain't that a big enough majority in any town?

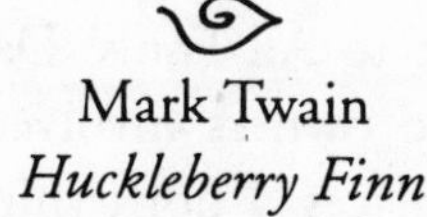

Mark Twain
Huckleberry Finn

T.S. Eliot thought that April was the cruelest month. He said it has something to do with lilacs being bred out of the dead land and memory mixing with desire, but I think the real reason is April Fool's Day. For 364 days a year most of us make perfectly good fools of ourselves without anyone paying us the least bit of attention. We religiously watch the O.J. trial and think that boxer Mike Tyson was a political prisoner. We watch daytime talk shows incessantly and read our horoscopes daily. Some of us deny the existence of the Holocaust. Then on All Fool's Day we devise tricks to be played on the particularly gullible among us.

The origins of April Fool's Day are obscure. It might derive from the March 25th feast of the Hilaria, a day of rejoicing and merriment in the Cybele-Attis cult once found in Greece and Rome. It is also not immediately obvious why the French call the fooled person a *poisson d' avril*, an April fish, while the Scots call the victim an April *gowk* (a cognate of "cuckoo"). What is becoming more apparent is that April

Fool's Day should be the feast day for *homo sapiens* as a whole. There is enough foolishness going around that almost all of us have a stake in marking the First of April as a special day. We ought to snip this day each year from the cloth of time, the way we celebrate the Fourth of July, or in the manner that some of us leave flowers pressed in the pages of family bibles. It should be a day of recognition that many of us in this life are on fools' errands.

The major problem with real foolishness, of course, is that we can't see it in ourselves. It is about as difficult as looking at one's own ears. It is much easier to find foolishness in others, particularly those in high places. Fools in high places are like people at the top of a mountain: everything looks small to them, and, without them knowing it, they look small to the rest of us.

I used to think it was purely accidental that the beginning of baseball season comes so close to All Fools' Day. Now I'm not so sure. Certainly both players and owners involved in the baseball dispute have many fools in high places. I don't think they realize how small they look to the rest of us.

Among the great western European monarchies there must have been a sense that foolishness regularly found its place at the side of the king and queen. I think that is why they had court jesters, a kind of palpable reminder of the capacity and the danger of royal foolishness. The baseball owners could use a court jester, too, and the players could have a designated jester, but just in the American League. Indeed, next year we should have opening day on All Fools' Day. The stands will be packed, and everyone will be thinking the day has been named after the other guy. The owners could market little jester dolls. They would sell millions of them.

Members of Congress these days are earnestly debating whether they any longer need a chaplain. Some might say it is foolish to dismiss the power of prayer, though it is clear that what they really need is a court jester. They could get him to explain how we are going to balance the budget, that way both sides could avoid the political fallout.

Aristotle thought that there is a foolish corner even in the heart of the sage. He believed the difference between the wise person and a fool is this: the foolishness of the fool is known to the world, but are hidden from himself, while the follies of the sage are known to himself and hidden from the world.

Aristotle was called many things in his life. *Un poisson d' avril* was not one of them.

Searching for a Verb

Verbs give one the most trouble in any language.

The New Heritage Dictionary

For the last several hours I have been searching for a verb. This exploration began when a dear friend abruptly ended our telephone conversations. Her young son had matter-of-factly announced to her, and by telephone extension to me, that a terrible accident had just transpired in the confines of the back yard of her small row house in Catonsville. It seems that a despicably foul fowl of some unknown variety had unleashed a well placed aerial assault on the newly baked cake the young mother had left to cool on a picnic table in the yard.

Thus, you can see my dilemma. How am I to describe the heinous activity of this inconsiderate bird? I know the French verb, but it somehow doesn't seem to fit. It most assuredly wasn't a pheasant or a French hen, I don't think they can fly. It was more likely a pigeon, given the tell-tale gastrointestinal clues left behind.

I could direct you to the proper page in *The American Heritage Dictionary of the English Language*. The predicate in question is listed here in its noun form. It does not, however, provide a picture. But even if I gave the suitable citation, people in some locales would still be confused. That particular dictionary, along with *Catcher in the Rye*, and a variety of other materials, is banned from public libraries in those jurisdictions. In these towns, it is said that half the traffic in dirty book stores these days are bad spellers and people with poor vocabularies sent there by their public librarians. In these dirty book stores, the dictionary is wrapped in brown paper, but you can find out what is sandwiched between "shirtwaist" and "shitzu."

But the subject of this essay is not the predicate—absent or otherwise. The real purpose of this discourse is to carefully analyze the boy's description of what occurred in the backyard. There are, even by the most conservative of estimates, tens of thousands of row houses in the greater Baltimore metropolitan area. Each of these row houses usually comes with some sort and size of backyard. On average, a Baltimore row house backyard is twenty feet by fifty feet, or 1,000 square feet. Now, even if the cake in question was one square foot, the chance of hitting this particular space is about ten million to one, or about the same odds as you and your car finding the only available parking space in Manhattan.

If we add to this the fact that my friend bakes only four cakes a year, then the chance of a cake being available for defilement are extremely small, increasing the odds that this was no accident.

This episode, of course, is the stuff of which conspiratorial theorists are made. When the boy arrives in college, he will need forty courses to graduate, and one of them is bound to be probability and statistics. After completing the course, he will more than likely begin to reflect on his childhood experiences. Eventually, his memory will come into clear focus on the incident with the bird. From that, we can inevitably expect another theory about the assassination of John F. Kennedy. And when that happens, it will be no accident.

For Sale: The Ten Commandments

We treat the ten commandments almost like they are recommendations or things to be bought and sold, things to be tailored to our own personal specifications like a pair of ill-fitting trousers or a set of false teeth.

Soren Kierkegaard
Journals

The Ten Commandments were sold the other day. By all accounts the bidding at Christie's was spirited. After an hour of brisk bids, the decalogue went to a senior partner in a New York law firm. It was not immediately apparent whether or not the firm represented another party who wished to remain anonymous in the transaction. Some insiders said Michael Jackson was the buyer, and that he believed the decalogue would look nice next to his Elephant Man collection, though Mr. Jackson's press secretary said the entertainer was unavailable for comment.

Perhaps the most exciting element to the bidding for the decalogue was the activity of a middle-aged man dressed in red spandex suit and matching satin cape. The man had arching eyebrows and spoke with a slight foreign accent. He insisted on using bidding number 666, though less than 100 people were issued numbers for the auction.

Some observers thought he was a member of a rock band, others that he was a professional wrestler. One unconfirmed news report suggested that the red-clad stranger was the entertainer formerly known as Prince. Whatever the man's identity, it is clear that he kept the bidding high, raising his number 666 on several occasions when the decalogue was about to be sold.

Another unconfirmed report circulating among observers at Christie's suggested that Donald Trump was the buyer of the Ten Commandments. He is reported to have told Christie's officials that he thought the decalogue would be a great investment, though he did not think he would keep all ten. Mr. Trump was unavailable for comment.

Still another unconfirmed rumor had Jim and Tammy Bakker reuniting after Mr. Bakker's parole. These anonymous sources suggested that the couple will reopen their religious theme park, with the decalogue playing an important role in the centerpieces of the renovated park's attractions, the "Mount Sinai Roller Coaster," and the "Crossing of the Red Sea Bumper Cars." A press spokesman for Mr. and Mrs. Bakker was unavailable for comment.

One final rumor began circulating at Christie's immediately following the sale. By late evening of the day of the auction, Ted Koppel had interviewed a professor of archeology at the Hebrew University in Jerusalem who claimed that the tablets sold at Christie's were forgeries. The professor pointed out that the auctioned decalogue was made of Plexiglas. Asked by Koppel if he thought the tablets were fakes, the professor responded, "You'd never be able to break those tablets over the head of a golden calf."

Later in his show, Mr. Koppel showed clips from a movie starring Charleton Heston. He pointed out that in the film Mr. Heston carries ten commandments down from Mount Sinai that look suspiciously like those auctioned at Christie's. But a spokesperson for Mr. Heston said the actor was unavailable for comment.

One issue left unresolved is whether the author of the Ten

Commandments will share in the profits from the $73,000 sale of the decalogue. Attorneys for Christie's were quick to point out that the tablets were authored well beyond the twenty-three year limit for international copyrights, and thus the content of the Ten Commandments is now within the public domain. Attorneys for the Almighty were unavailable for comment.

Chapter

Five

On Good and Evil

The perception of Good and Evil—whatever choices we may make—is the first requisite of a spiritual life.

T.S. Eliot

Much of my life is now spent mulling over moral matters. One of the great surprises in my life of teaching, however, is how little attention professional philosophers give to applying moral theory to everyday ethical dilemmas. In this chapter, we explore a few of these conundrums: Holocaust denial; the inevitability of war; and the contemporary absence in this country of what might reasonably be called moral discourse.

Moral Ambiguity and Necessary Evil

If we will not be peaceable, let us then at least be honest, acknowledge that we continue to slaughter one another, not because Christianity permits it, but because we reject its laws.

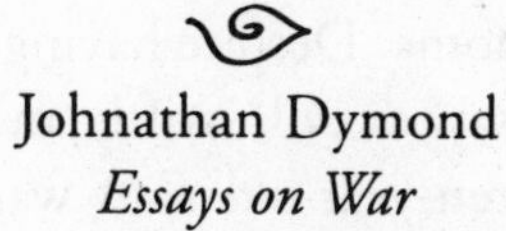

Johnathan Dymond
Essays on War

Let there be no violence in religion.
If one believes in Islam, he must be so directed.

Mohammed
The Koran

When I was a boy of ten I lived in a working class neighborhood full of fathers who dirtied their hands at work and mothers who bore little if any resemblance to June Cleaver even on her worst days. Small boys settled their disputes with their fists. I was one of the bigger boys in the neighborhood. Every now and then I was called on to aid one or another of my smaller or younger friends who had fallen victim to Frankie, a child full of sorrow and animosity who seemed to take great comfort in the suffering he inflicted on others.

Every few months or so I would talk to Frankie about his treatment of the smaller boys. But after he continued on his usual bloody course, I was called upon to flatten his nose—extracting blood for blood.

For myself and those around me Frankie was as close as we had come to genuine evil. He was possessed of a kind of incorrigibility, haunted with a hatred we had not seen in our first ten years on the planet. Frankie was angry and sometimes sullen, but he never cried, not even in the middle of a fight.

What I wish to tell you about is my walks home from fighting Frankie in the vacant lot filled with shattered glass and broken down 1950s automobiles. I want to tell you how the smaller boys, all victims of Frankie's, would call him derisive names. After Frankie's trouncing, they jeered and mocked him and I usually joined them.

But inside myself, deep inside in that private place where even ten-year-old boys hope and fear, in that secret shelter, I always would feel ashamed on those walks home. Despite having done the good, despite having dealt with what I saw as evil, swiftly and surely, I felt ashamed. What took seed in my ten-year-old soul was a sense of the moral ambiguity that comes with meeting violence with violence even when it was a strike at incorrigible evil.

Human beings are like balls of string. Life is little more than the rolling out. We all roll out, some longer than others. None of us is ever in just one place. We inhabit a series of places including all we have been. My string has rolled out another three decades or so since my bloody encounters with Frankie. But I am still made of the same string. Today my string is knotted with the moral ambiguities of thirty years. It is knotted with the memory of high school classmates whose lives took nineteen years to grow and a few moments in rice patties in Indo-China to come to an end. Their strings were cut quickly, unmercifully, before their strings had much of a chance to roll out.

Now there are a few more knots to tie with string cut too soon. We have just begun to bring back the frayed cord of young lives lost in the Persian Gulf. And at the center of these knots we tie is that same moral ambiguity I sensed as a ten-year-old child trying to vanquish neighborhood evil.

In the meantime, both sides speak of God being on their side. In my heart I am certain that war is not a swift judgment from God as the simple rhetoric would have us believe. Rather, war is a crucifixion for both sides and another nailing to the cross of the God of love.

As Martin Luther King, Jr., observed, "We live in a time of guided missiles and misguided men." We will defeat Sadaam Hussein, after having laid waste to mothers, and brothers, and sisters, and fathers on both sides. Afterwards, we will once again succumb to that erroneous belief that life will have been made safer. We will hold this belief even more fervently because we vanquish what is seen as irredeemable evil. May God forgive us for this, even if we see it as necessary. But if those actions are necessary, may we at least have the courage to call them by their proper name: necessary evils.

Dressing for Armageddon

The sole purpose of an education is to know a good person when we see one.

William James
Talks to Teachers

Halloween. All Hallows' Eve, a holy evening when the souls of the dead were thought to roam the earth, some returning to expectant loved-ones, while others affected long-awaited revenge. The dead wandered among the living until the evening of the following day, All Hallows, what is now called All Saints' Day. Then, promptly at sundown, the shades returned whence they came, having provided a twenty-four hour reminder of the ubiquitous human need to make the invisible visible.

Among the ancient Celts, October 31st was the feast of Sambain, New Year's Eve. The feast was a fire festival where huge conflagrations turned the Irish and Scottish hills into fiery mountains, a kind of fire insurance erected to ward off the return of menacing spirits with perfect recall.

Later the Celtic Sambain became the Christian All Hallows' Eve, and the bonfire became a convenient way of convincing the Celts that conversion to the true church was decidedly in their self-interest. On

All Hallows' Day, 1755, the Lisbon earthquake struck with such a fury that by the end of the day the world had 40,000 newly restless souls to appease the following Halloween. On the next day, those who survived the Lisbon holocaust began burning heretics in impressive *autos da fe* designed to divine the cause and cure for God's great shaking of the earth. Historians tell us that the smoke from the bonfires was visible over most of the Iberian peninsula.

In those earlier times, people seemed so much clearer about what evil was and where it might be found, but they had not yet managed many of the impressive technological advancements that make our age so good at killing. We live in an age when the demons can't always be so easily distinguished from the rest of us. Unlike those who burned witches at the stake, with modern weaponry we often cannot see far enough to watch the demons as they die. Perhaps this is another reason why our century has been so much better at killing each other than those who came before us.

In my own 1950s childhood, Halloween was a time to dress like the evil ones: itchy plastic masks and black cotton suits, complete with a matching set of painted patellas, femurs, and phalanges; red satin satans with runny mascara and runny noses; and bed sheets transformed into replicas of a friendly ghost whose regular visitations could be seen all year long on Saturday morning cartoons.

Our 1950s depictions of evil seem so benign now at least until we understand that somebody's fathers and mothers were aiming nuclear warheads in those years at Soviet cities across eastern Europe and Asia. The parents of Soviet children were aiming them back at us. Every year around All Hallows' Eve, in grade schools all over America, children were taught something called "duck and cover"—a maneuver that involved crawling under our wooden and wrought-iron desks during atomic bomb practice and waiting for the "all clear" sign.

In the third grade I dressed as a devil for Halloween. Each morning we dutifully assembled for eight o'clock mass and proceeded *en masse* to the section reserved for the fifty or so members of my class. I felt more than a bit guilty that Halloween morning when my devil's tail went swishing up to the communion railing. At least I knew enough to keep my red pitch fork back in the pew.

That afternoon didn't go nearly as well. In the middle of parading our costumes before envious and costume-less girls in blue jumpers and boys with blue clip-on ties—children with mothers devoid of imagination and a knack with cardboard—the horn for atomic bomb practice went off. I remember taking off my devil gloves and biting my fingernails, while waiting for Armageddon. Huddled under my desk, I prayed while staring at the wrought-iron feet that looked too much like cloven hoofs. My little red horns pressed to the shinny linoleum floor, I did not pray that the world would be saved.

I prayed only that God would be able to tell the good guys from the bad ones.

A Dearth of Discourse

Testimony is a bit like an arrow shot from a long bow; its force depends on the strength of the hand that draws it. But argument is like an arrow from a crossbow, which has equal force no matter who draws it.

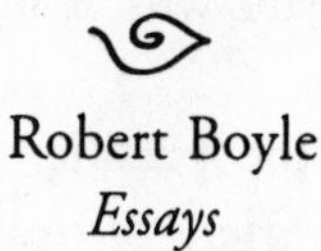

Robert Boyle
Essays

Lately I have had a number of rather heated political conversations with myself in the privacy of my own head. Sometimes I talk to myself to find out what I am thinking. It is like a small boy turning his pockets inside out to discover what exactly is in them. One begins to find all sorts of musings—personal property that somehow remained unaccounted for in the general neural inventory.

I happened on one of these pieces this morning while rummaging through my collection of half-thoughts. It's an odd conviction, one that I have not yet uttered, and so it remains something I can put back where it came from if necessary. The conviction is this: political debate in America is no longer like a hard-fought tennis match, where one returns the opponents best serve.

Contemporary political discussions in this country are now more like a round of golf, where one goes on hitting the ball until all the holes are played. Political debate has been replaced by a series of well-orchestrated anecdotes accompanied by saber-rattling where it seems to the media manipulators to be appropriate.

There is a genuine dearth of political discourse in American public life. I have noticed this lately while listening to George Bush explain exactly why we are in Saudi Arabia. Daniel Schorr, James Reston, and others recently have pointed out that Bush seems to be attempting to be all things for all people and so he is not really enough of anything to be a something.

Bush reminds me of the description in Rainer Maria Rilke's *Notebooks of Malte Laurids Brigge* of those people who change their faces with such rapidity that they quickly run out of personae and then have to walk around with what Rilke calls the "no face" showing through.

Why is it that we can't have reasoned political debate in this country—not just about the Middle East, but about abortion, capital punishment, or a tax increase? And why is it that so few people seem to notice?

Mr. Bush does not look too presidential. He looks more like an indecisive man trying on a variety of ties in his dressing room to see how the rest of the world will think he looks. If Rilke's protean character disappoints us, we can always put down the book. But how do we do that with a president, particularly if he skillfully has been created to reflect all our disparate images of him.

This lack of substance is not something peculiar to our commander-in-chief. A few weeks ago, Richard B. Cheney, the secretary of defense, told the assembled troops in Saudi Arabia that we are there to defend "American values." Somewhat later, while George Bush was attending the first anniversary celebration of the Czech Republic's "velvet revolution," the president declared: "Fundamental freedoms are threatened by the crisis in the Persian Gulf." Between these two events, the Saudi government announced passage of a law prohibiting women, native or foreign, from driving cars in its country.

In This Season of Peace, is Peace Possible?

In the arts of peace, man is a bungler.

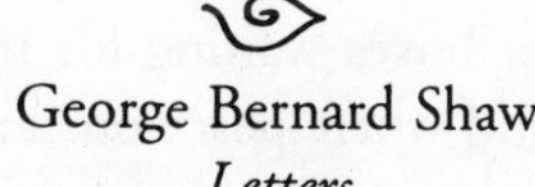

George Bernard Shaw
Letters

There is something unnatural about parents burying their children.

Herodotus
The Histories

The Roman deity Janus was a curious, metaphysical creature. He was represented with two faces, joined along the line from ear to jaw. The two countenances simultaneously surveyed the past and future, one keenly aware of history, the other possessed of a kind of pristine foreknowledge. It is not surprising that the Romans associated Janus with time. But they also saw in this two-faced god a symbol of war.

As we approach Christmas, I am thinking about this most curious of Roman deities. I've become convinced that we all share with Janus this ability to look in opposite directions. I am wondering if my vision of the past isn't much better than my view of the future.

Last year at this time I wrote an essay about a short walk I took in the woods with a three-year-old boy. We went looking for holly. In the essay, I reminisced about my childhood, about how the Cold War hung over these holidays like an invisible Grinch, ready to steal Christmas and everything else.

This time last year events in Germany and eastern Europe had convinced me that peace was about to break out all over, just in time for the season of peace. I know now that my proclamations of universal peace were more than a bit premature. The remains of Flight 103 are scattered across the Scottish countryside in this season of peace and brotherhood. These are hills where I have walked many times.

So now I wonder about the boy as this Christmas approaches, and I wonder about Christmases to come. Will his world be like the world of my childhood? Will he live in a world, as I did, that looks too much like a collection of tinder boxes waiting for the proper match? Will this boy ever live in a world where peace on earth is not simply something to be sung about at holiday season?

Here in the dead of night, my eye to the future is not as clear as Janus's. It cannot see the future; it cannot tell what sort of world the young boy will be required to make sense of; it only clearly apprehends the notion that we are one of the only species that gratuitously kills its own members—for oil, for land, or sometimes for a pair of basketball sneakers.

When the Hurly-Burly's Done

Battle between man and man, tribe and tribe, village, state, and nation regarded by the unthinking as abnormal or aberrant behavior, has been, historically, the norm.

Hanson Baldwin
Battles Lost and Won

William Shakespeare chooses to open his tragedy *Macbeth* with a question posed by one of the three witches: "When shall we meet again?" The second witch's answer: "When the Hurly-Burly's done, when the battle's lost and won."

The world's 128 nations must meet again now that the second witch's condition, and those of George Bush, have been met. The allies have vanquished their foe. And in the eyeblink that has been our stay on the planet, we see ourselves as the victors. We understand ourselves as those who have heroically brought good out of evil. The President said as much in his speech declaring victory over the Iraqis. The world is once again ready for peace and we have made it that way.

The ancient Egyptians thought that twilight would never come on their day in the sun. The Greeks suffered from a similar attack of necessary hubris. Archeologists have spent the last century or so digging up the remains of these immortal civilizations, dead now thousands of years. One day America, too, will be just another strata in the archeologists' excavations. What will they say of us in a thousand years? What will archeologists of the future conclude about our culture?

They will say that we were noble, courageous, and kind. But they will add that we were myopic in our moral vision. They will say that we did what we thought was right. But they will also conclude that we had a penchant for destroying what we could not control.

They will probably not ask if this was a just war, particularly if our end comes with a bang and not a whimper. They will not be impressed with our conditions for a just war, but rather with the fact that we had so many of them.

The archeologists, I should think, will take the long view of history—a perspective that places this moment of American euphoria in its larger deadly context. For them, this war will have lasted the length of a heartbeat when measured against the backdrop of all human history.

Iraqis and Kuwaitis, Palestinians and Jews, Americans and Russians will all be put together. We will be given a single place somewhere in an unbroken line of violence stretching back to the Sumerians. We will be measured by our likenesses. We will all have blood on our hands. These archeologists of the future will, more than likely, be unconcerned about the winners and losers in this war and those that preceded it. They will perhaps marvel at the horror and perversity that war took in our time.

And if this unbroken line of violence were to come to an abrupt end, it will not, in all likelihood, be a peaceful one.

These future archeologists probably will muse that we thought each of our wars would be the last. We always thought we were fighting for peace. We believed there would be a new world order and that each war was the war to end all wars.

And if these sifters of history look back on one last war, on Armageddon, the irony will not be lost.

When the Holocaust is Denied

There are thousands hacking at the branches of evil
to one who is striking at the root.

Henry David Thoreau
The Journals

There is in this country and in Britain, France, and even in Germany and Austria, a vocal and sometimes oddly effective collection of strange ideological bedfellows who believe there was no Holocaust. These revisionists, as they prefer to be called, make a half-dozen or so principal claims which include, but are not limited to, the following:

- There was no mass, intentional killing of the Jews by the Nazis.

- Stories about millions of Jews being killed in portable carbon monoxide trucks and later with Zyklon B in various killing centers were a hoax.

- The "final solution" was actually a plan to expel Jews from Western Europe and return them to eastern Europe, whence they came.

- The number of Jews and others killed in concentration camps numbered between 200,000 and 300,000. The figures for Auschwitz, the deniers say, are no more than 50,000.

- The genocide myth was invented by Allied authorities in concert with Zionists who wished to turn manufactured European guilt into pressure for establishing the post-war state of Israel.

In addition to these larger claims, there are many more specific ones that, in their own way, are just as pernicious: that the diary of Anne Frank was a fake; that the Nuremberg trials, like the Stalin show trials, were among the great kangaroo courts of all time; that survivors of the Nazi death camps were mistaken about what they saw, heard, and felt; and, still worse, that the survivors lied.

A November 1992 study published in the Italian newspaper *L'espresso* and reprinted in the *New York Times* suggests that ten percent of Italians have serious doubts that the Holocaust occurred. Last spring, a Roper poll published in the *Boston Globe* indicated that one of three Americans believes it is possible that the Holocaust never took place. In France, the leader of the extreme-right National Front, Jean-Marie Le Pen, said in a 1987 interview: "I do not say that the gas chambers didn't exist. I could not see them . . . But I think this is a minute detail of the Second World War." In 1986, representatives of the Institute for Historical Review, the euphonic name for the chief organization of American Holocaust deniers, testified before Congress and urged that their materials be included in the public school curriculum.

At first this may seem akin to inviting Flat Earth Society members or people who believe the moon landing was a hoax to appear at a congressional hearing on the space program budget. Generally speaking, however, people believe the world is flat not because they hate other people, but rather from sheer silliness. Many of them have tongues planted firmly in cheeks. There is not, however, a fun-loving quirkiness in denying that the Holocaust occurred. These people are deadly serious, and that is what makes them so dangerous.

How are rational women and men of good will to respond to these deniers? Ought we to marshal the evidence against them? Ought we assemble the billions of documents, the extraordinary paper trail stained with the blood of innocent children, in order to show these people they are indisputably wrong?

Ought we to show them the empty Zyklon B canisters, or the rooms at Auschwitz full of toothbrushes, eating utensils, clothes hangers and suitcases—all tiny but integral reminders of nearly six million vanished lives?

Shall we show them the room containing 4,000 pounds of human hair? Shall we show them the report from chief chemist Jan Robel of the Institute for Forensic Medicine in Krakow, to whom ten pounds of hair was sent in May 1945 for chemical analysis? His test results noted the presence of cyanide, the leading agent in Zyklon B, in every follicle analyzed.

Should we make them examine the blueprints for the Auschwitz showers which revealed that, although every room contained twenty shower heads, there were no water lines leading into these buildings?

I must confess I do not know the answers to these questions. A direct response is a kind of tacit admission that there is an argument here. Yet ignoring the deniers may mislead some into believing that the revisionists' objections cannot be answered. The deniers remind me of Voltaire's Dr. Pangloss, who, in the face of overwhelming evidence of heinous crimes and unspeakable acts, continues to maintain that "this is the best of all possible worlds." (We must remember, of course, that Pangloss's name comes from the Greek "all tongue.")

Historians tell us the United States engaged in a war with Spain from April 25 to July 25, 1898. The Spanish-American War featured five major engagements, two by sea and three by land. The total number of combatants did not exceed 10,000. Far more on both sides died of disease than the 398 Spaniards and 217 Americans killed in combat. No known participants are living from either side, and by the standards of Nazi Germany, both sides were shoddy record keepers.

So why is it that no one denies the existence of the Spanish-

American War, while some are intent on denying the Holocaust, a series of events extending over half a decade, directly involving eight to ten million people (many still alive), and chronicled by the best record keepers on earth?

Sometimes what Holocaust denial involves is pure ignorance. As Philip Hallie points out in *Lest Innocent Blood Be Shed*, sometimes evil is not produced by the diabolical. Rather, it is a kind of byproduct of stupidity. But more often, it is something more pernicious. Most often Holocaust deniers simply cannot countenance any view but their own. There is an irrationality that must be dealt with seriously by the academic community.

Holocaust denial is also intimately related to the worst kind of dissembling that attempts to hide its face of hate behind a mask of scholarship and the eyeglasses of critical and dispassionate analysis.

Although these people have a right to speak, they do not have the right to speak in my classroom. Where they do have the right to speak, they should also be expected to be exposed for what they are. This means, of course, that informed people of good will have a duty not to be silent.

Pierre Vidal-Naquet aptly labeled the deniers "assassins of memory." It is memory that gives the events of the Holocaust ontological status. The Holocaust exists because we refuse to forget. We must not, therefore, allow these revisionists, whether ill-tended or not, to murder six million human beings a second time.

We Interrupt This Christmas Dance

Christmas: It is always such a mixing of this world and the next—
but that, after all, is the idea.

Evelyn Underhill
The Letters

In the morning, they danced, the small boy and his father, spinning and laughing, all the while holding tightly to each other, as though they clung to life itself. One after another, Christmas tunes played with the slow waltz of "Silent Night" giving way to the hectic whirl of "Jingle Bells." They moved from room to room, gliding through air full of pine and innocence.

The father held the boy tightly. He pressed the baby's cheek to his mouth. Christmas and all the man remembered about it suddenly became a possession, something secret and private, like few other things he had ever owned. Christmas and all that it used to mean sat in the man's heart, waiting forever, like immortality—something beautiful and foreign, beyond all that he now thought of as real.

The man wished it were snowing. He longed for a magical event, where enchantment is sent to Earth in the form of white snowflakes and an only son. He wished for the world to be covered in white, so that the baby boy could see nothing but the silence and purity that comes with a great snowfall.

The man opened his eyes. He peered out the window, half expecting the snow. Instead, he caught a glimpse of the mail truck, in a small cloud of smoke, pulling away from the box by the side of the road.

Amid the green and red Christmas greetings, they found the single white envelope without a return address. The man, a writer, had seen his share of these letters. Even unopened, they send a small shudder through the system. His premonition was right.

Earlier in the month, the man had written a piece about the dangers of Holocaust denial. The letter was a response. The opening line was enough: "How did those kikes get you to tell their lies for them???" It was, of course, unsigned.

The man's eyes darted down the page full of underlinings and multiple exclamation points. The father shifted the squirming baby to his other hip and got the last line on the bleached white paper: "Hitler only made one mistake—he didn't kill all of them!!!"

The air had turned cold, and the man took the shivering baby back into the house. They warmed themselves by the fire, and the father dropped the letter on the burning logs. It turned brown at the corners and then disappeared. The anonymous writer is out there somewhere. The man gathers by a line near the bottom, a line about Jews being "the killers of our Lord," that the composer fancies himself as a Christian.

The man wonders if the writer has danced with his own baby. He wonders if the writer has taught the baby to love Jesus, a Jew, and then to think, the way he does, about all other Jews. The man remembers a line from the philosopher Soren Kierkegaard about how most Christians are willing to follow the admonition to love others—as long as they get to pick their own exceptions.

In the afternoon, the baby falls asleep, and the man begins to write. He writes about a corrosiveness of adulthood that forces us to make the better parts of ourselves inaccessible to all except those with whom we are most intimate. The man hopes that on a sacred day, like Christmas, the writer of the letter can love at least those who are close to him.

A while later, the baby awakens, and the man and the child resume their dance. They whirl and spin. They share that laugh that only comes when one tickles the ribs of a small child. A moment later, they look out the window beyond the oak trees to the great pines that line the property. The sky is a bright gray. The boy smells of pine and baby shampoo. And the man could swear it is snowing.

The Mystery of Evil

The Belief in a supernatural source of evil is not necessary; men alone are quite capable of every wickedness.

Joseph Conrad
The Heart of Darkness

The fundamental question about evil, at least in so far as the effect it has on *homo sapiens*, is why human beings do such terrible things to each other. The admission of Jeffrey Dahmer that he murdered at least seventeen young men in his Milwaukee apartment serves as another macabre reminder that the explanatory tools used to unlock the mystery of evil have been, for the most part, blunt instruments, trying to do the work of delicate, refined tools—tools that may not even exist.

Theology, biology, philosophy, anthropology, sociology, and, of course, psychology, all have attempted to come to grips with the phenomena of evil, but it takes only a cursory reading of the news reports of the arrest of Dahmer, or a few minutes watching *Silence of the Lambs*, to understand that the intellectual rubrics we have devised for explaining evil pale when laid alongside the power of the mystery they propose to domesticate.

One of the major difficulties in understanding evil is that we shift rather uneasily from the use of "evil" as a noun, to the employment of the word as an adjective. In western culture we seem not to be able to make up our minds about whether evil is a thing, or whether it is best understood as description for a number of disparate acts that have as their common core the infliction of unnecessary suffering.

Another related question about evil is whether its province is metaphysics or psychopathology. In traditional formulations of ethical theory and jurisprudence, one is ordinarily held responsible for his actions if he knew what he was doing, intended to do it, and had the ability to keep from doing it.

The Jeffrey Dahmer story, as well as the less sensational John Hinkley case, remind us just how difficult to determine with any certainty exactly what a person's mental state is at the time of a crime.

Indeed, it is significant that after John Hinkley was found innocent by reason of insanity, protests were heard from a number of quarters, both private and governmental, against allowing this ostensibly sick man the experience of a heavily-guarded leave with his family. Given our public attitudes about evil, it is unlikely that we will ever refrain from calling Jeffrey Dahmer evil, even if he were declared innocent by reason of insanity.

Questions about the definition, etiology, and responsibility for evil are not the only ones the Dahmer revelations call to mind. There is also the question about why this story fascinates us so.

Evil characters—whether they are found in fiction or in our daily newspapers—are something to which many of us are clearly drawn. Nineteenth-century German theologian Rudoph Otto spoke of the transcendent as simultaneously "mysterious, tremendous, and fascinating." He thought it was at once attractive and yet repulsive, and clearly the same can be said about our modern attitudes toward evil. Carl Jung was convinced that the peculiar charm of evil comes from the possession by each of us of something he called the "shadow self." In Jung's view, the shadow projects qualities and impulses that we most fear in ourselves onto others who can then be hated for their evilness. Although this explanation, and countless other psychodynamic approaches, have some merit, they tend to ignore the very real evil of the acts of Jeffrey Dahmer, by suggesting that our complex attitudes toward him are nothing more than mere projections.

What we can learn about evil is to be found in great pieces of fiction. Joseph Conrad's *Heart of Darkness* and Fyodor Dostoyevsky's *Crime and Punishment*, both written well before contemporary social-scientific literature on evil, point to the notion that our fascination about evil is at once an attraction to external power and an abiding curiosity about what we are like at our most fundamental level. More importantly, both Conrad and Dostoyevsky seem to leave open the answer to that question about our basic human nature.

Perhaps in the final analysis, the wisest thing to be said about evil by those writing in social-scientific and philosophical journals these days is an observation made a few years ago by Mary Midgley, a contemporary British philosopher. She writes:

> I first entered this jungle myself some time ago, by slipping out over the wall of the tiny arid garden cultivated at that time under the name of British Moral Philosophy. I did so in an attempt to think about human nature and the problem of evil. The evils in the world, I thought, are real. That they are so is neither a fancy imposed on us by our own culture, nor one created by our will and imposed on the world. Such suggestions are bad faith.

The Devil at Our Elbows

I am not surprised at the idea of the devil being always at our elbows. Those who invented him no doubt could not conceive how people could be so atrocious to one another, without the intervention of a fiend.

Horace Walpole
Letters

This is not the first time I had seen pictures of that distraught fire fighter carrying the lifeless baby. I had seen before the aftermath of such "political statements." Christmas of 1979 I was in the Bologna train station an hour before it was blown to bits by the Red Brigade. I had sat on the same bench whose splintered remains were later spread across the front pages of all the Italian newspapers. I had played peek-a-boo with a toddler on that bench. I had smiled at her mother and grandmother. They all surely were lost in the blast. They were country people who had come to the big city for the Christmas holiday. I'm sure they knew very little about Italian politics and "wars of liberation."

Four years later, again, at Christmas time, I was on my way to Harrod's in London. I had reached the Princess Street tube station when a blast rocked the underground. When I arrived at street level, the god Pan had struck: all I could see was splintered glass, and the body of a dead dog who had walked down the wrong street at the right time. At the end of the street I could see a twisted baby's pram. The Irish Republican Army had detonated a bomb on the ground floor of Harrod's department store a few days before Christmas. I assume the baby was inside. The telephone caller who later claimed responsibility for the blast called it "an act of liberation." The baby did not live long enough to know that adult English people often hate the Irish, and adult Irish people hate them back.

I thought about these dead children upon hearing the news that a bomb ripped apart the federal building in Oklahoma City. I thought about the mother who had spent the weekend before the Oklahoma blast shopping for the right pair of sneakers for her five-year-old, a child at the day care center in the Murrah Building. They found the sneakers after the blast, but found no trace of the little girl.

I thought about the child who took the day off from the same day care center to spend it with her grandparents. The grandfather made the mistake that day of visiting the Social Security Office in the same building. The man made the horrible mistake of bringing his wife and grandchild along . They all are gone. It is unlikely that the child knew much about the second amendment or what a militia is.

A little while later, while waiting for my nine-year-old's school bus to arrive, I thought about the children caught in the inferno at the Branch Davidian complex in Waco, Texas. These children knew nothing of what was going on. They, too, died that way. As the bus arrived, my son asked if it was safe for him to go to school. I hesitated for a moment, thinking about what a dangerous place the world has become, and then I told him that nothing would happen to him.

Later, while driving to work, I tried to listen to the National Public Radio accounts of the Oklahoma City investigation. My mind drifted, like a small boat whose single tether has been pulled from its moorings. Suddenly I began thinking about Fyodor Dostoyevsky's *The Brothers Karamazov*. In the book Ivan, an intellectual, argues with his brother Alyosha about the suffering of innocent children. Of the suffering of adults, "of the other tears of humanity with which the earth is soaked from its crust to its center," Ivan will not comment. He suggests that adults are so often themselves to blame. They have stolen fire from the gods. They have eaten from the fruit of the tree of the knowledge of good and evil, and thus are so frequently themselves to blame. "But then there are the children," Ivan asks, "what am I to do about them?"

Ivan goes on to tell his younger brother, a seminary student, that if God's plan allows for the suffering of even a single child, and if Ivan's own salvation could only be effected through the suffering of that solitary child, then Ivan would "hasten to return his entrance ticket."

Now it is late in the evening and I cannot stop thinking about the dead children, and about Ivan Karamazov. I can't stop thinking that if there is a divine plan, it is a tragic one. But if there is no plan, then life takes place in a silent universe, one filled only with self-conscious protoplasm and chance.

I turn off the light in my study. In the darkness of the hallway, I kick a small object left by my two-year-old in the course of his day's activities. I bend down to pick up the object.

It was a single untied green sneaker.

Chapter

Six

On Fathering

Every noble youth looks back, as to the chiefest joy which this world's honor ever gave him, to the moment when first he saw his father's eyes flash with pride.

John Ruskin

The craft of fathering is much more difficult than anything else I have ever accomplished. It requires the wisdom of Solomon, the patience of Job (at least the Job of the prose), and the decisive abilities of a triage surgeon. Fathering is also the most exhilarating and rewarding thing I have ever done. In these pieces I tell something of the small epiphanies that come with the fathering of two small boys—little centers of energy that seem always to be bursting onto the scene.

Father's Day Times Two

There are to us no ties at all in just being a father.
A son is distinctly an acquired taste.

Heywood Broun
Pieces of Hate

Stepfather. It is an unfortunate word. It conjures up the image of Hamlet's white-hot hatred of Claudius, or a male version of Cinderella's domestic situation. *Bartlett's Quotations* has fifty-eight entries under father. None for stepfather. *Webster's New 20th Century Dictionary* points out that one of the meanings of stepchild was a synonym for orphan. Stepchild comes from the Anglo-Saxon word *astepon*, the verb "to bereave." It's not too difficult to figure out why we don't use the prefix in our house.

I met my son (he is not my biological son) when he was nearly three years old. When I married his mother a year later, he managed to find enough room in his heart to call two very different men Daddy. It was the boy's idea. His natural father was not so sure about sharing the title. Eventually, he relented. I don't know how he decided that "father" is not something that dissipates if shared. I'm not so sure I could have been as magnanimous.

I don't steal glances at my son to decide if he has my hair or cheekbones. I find myself staring at this child because I can't imagine loving the boy any more than I do. I don't get to make puffy claims about how his baby pictures look like mine, or how he hits a baseball like I did in Little League. I feel a bit sheepish, even guilty, when a stranger at the supermarket insists that the boy favors me. I can sense that these moments are awkward for the boy. I can only guess what thoughts, what difficult and complicated allegiances, tug at his small soul on Father's Day. I am only beginning to understand that it takes a special kind of courage to be a boy with two fathers.

James Joyce in *Ulysses* suggests that for a boy, a father is a "necessary evil." John Steinbeck once remarked that "father and son are natural enemies and each is happier and more secure in keeping it that way." Franz Kafka seems to have built an entire literary career on the awesome attraction and repulsion of his father, Hermann. I read these men more carefully now. I search for clues in their lives. I practice a kind of magical thinking where, if I can pinpoint the problems in their relationships with their fathers, some keys to explain it all, this kind of unhealable fracture will not happen to my son and me, or the boy and his natural father.

Friedrich Nietzsche's father died when he was four. Much later, he wrote, "When a boy has not had a good father, he must create one." I always think about this line on Father's Day—the longing and desperation it implies. But I wonder what Nietzsche might have said about my son, a boy with two men trying, in different ways, to be good fathers.

The boy has recently turned six. He had two birthday parties. Both fathers attend his Little League games. Each of us has reassured the boy in the middle of the night. We both have felt the small arrows a wounded four-year-old can pluck at the soft tissue of the heart. I wonder if his other dad thinks about the inevitable separation and the tender pain that will come later on. I wonder if we both will worry about the rebellion. And I wonder if we will have the good sense to keep from blaming it on the other father.

From very early on, I thought about my own father as old, or at the very least as middle-aged. The astonishing truth was that my father was then a man much younger than I am now. My father is in his mid-sixties. He has worked all his life with his hands. Last week, while I was struggling with this essay, while I was trying to make some sense out of what it means to be a father, my father showed up to put a roof on the small shed next to our house. Looking out the window, I could watch him work. There were the same deft movements, the same sureness of purpose that I saw as his unwilling and unappreciative employee in my high school summers.

Row after row, he laid down interlocking gray shingles. Each row, only partially covering the row before it. Each row interlocking with the next, keeping out the wind and weather. It did not occur to me until that morning how much my family is like those rows of shingles. Each generation fastened and supported to the whole by the one before it. But I wonder how my son regularly manages to find his place, interlocked in two very different families.

I wanted to tell my father that I was trying to write about all this. I was attempting to write about all that had passed for forty-one years between the two of us, things that have remained, for the most part, unarticulated. I wanted to tell him about the things that have passed from him, through me, to this boy he has come to love. I went out to the shed to tell him, but he had finished his job and was gone.

What I wanted to tell him was that I now understand that when it comes to the word "father," it is so much easier to be a verb than a noun. I wanted to tell him that as a young man I was wrong for blaming him for failing to be perfect and that what was important was the love and unexpressed pride that still passes between us silently, but as real as a whispered prayer. More than anything, I wanted to tell him that someday I want my son to feel the same way about both his fathers as I do about mine.

I wanted to tell my father, but he had finished his job and was gone.

Future Perfect

There is always one moment in childhood
when the door opens and lets in the future.

Graham Greene
The Power and the Glory

It was the flashing yellow lights on the small red box that first attracted the five-year-old boy. He and the man were on the way out of the diner when they stopped to examine the box, complete with the picture of a gypsy grinning from behind her silver ball.

"What does the machine do?" asked the boy. "It tells the future," said the man. "If you put a quarter in the slot and place your hand here, on the top of the machine, it will tell you your future."

The boy tried to stretch his dimpled fingers to fill the outline of the large hand painted on the flat surface of the machine. His small fingers covered only two of the five metal electrodes protruding from the tips of each of the machine's painted fingers. The boy worried about his hand not being big enough for a real future, so the man placed his right hand over the boy's, now covering all the crucial electrodes.

"Will it still be my future?" the boy inquired anxiously. "It will still be your future," the man replied.

The father placed a quarter in the machine. For a moment, nothing happened. Then the machine began to make a mysterious humming sound. The boy's eyes brightened as a small filament inside the crystal ball began to glow.

A moment later, the machine was printing out the five-year-old's future. With all the solemnity the occasion warranted, the man read the words gliding across the face of the machine. "You should be careful this week," the man intoned, "when making serious financial commitments."

For a long moment the boy stood silently, staring at the machine. "Does that mean I'm going to have a good day?" he inquired. "That means you are going to have a great day," the father said. They walked out of the diner holding hands.

On the way to pre-school, the man stole small glances in the rear-view mirror at the boy having a great day. After dropping him off and watching the extra little bounce in the boy's step as he moved toward the large gray door that led to his future, the father thought about that old bromide that the future holds no guarantees.

He knew it holds a few.

Original Sin

Tis the faith that launched point-blank her dart
at the head of a lie, Original Sin.

Robert Browning
Gold Hair: A Story of Pornic

The five-year-old boy looked squarely into his father's eyes and said, "No, I won't eat the broccoli."

The father sat opposite the boy. The man's long right arm stretched across the white kitchen table. The useful end of the arm came to an insistent point of the index finger that tapped the table next to the green vegetable in question.

"If you don't eat the broccoli," the man heard himself saying, "then you won't grow up to be big and strong." For a moment, the man thought he heard an echo in the room, or perhaps it was another room, where a 1950s General Electric refrigerator could be heard humming in the background.

A moment later, the man thought that for the first time he now had a real understanding of the concept of original sin. It consists entirely in the genetic propensity to act more and more like one's parents, despite all one's best efforts to avoid doing so, until one is hardly distinguishable from them in certain apparently important matters. The eating habits, or the absence of eating habits, among small children is clearly one of those matters. Because of original sin, certain things involuntarily pop out of a father's mouth despite his earlier insistence that such stupid and inane things would never be said to his children.

The boy looked across the table at the man. His five-year-old fingers, wrapped around an adult fork, were poised above the greens.

"I don't want to be big and strong."

The boy placed the fork beside his plate and folded his arms so that the dimples at his elbows disappeared. The man felt an almost involuntary shuffling of emotional cards going on in the middle of his head, or was it his heart? His parents had unsuccessfully played most of these card thirty-five years before. The man had already tried the ones marked "guilt" and "shame." They had worked no better than had "growing up to be big and strong."

The man knew he had one last card to play. He found himself thinking about the boy's former nanny, Monica, a woman of almost preternatural kindness and patience. Earlier in the evening the boy's mother had mentioned that after supper they would call long distance to the much-missed Monica.

The man sat uneasily, his index finger in retreat, as the last dangerous card lay suspended on the tip of his tongue. There is almost always that moment—before even the most gentle of woundings—where reason tries desperately to catch up with habit and emotion. It almost always seems to fail.

"If you don't eat your broccoli," the man insisted, his finger stabbing the air above the formica separating them, "you will not be able to speak with Monica when we call her later this evening." As the last words of the sentence left his mouth, he instantly wanted them back. But a card played is a card played.

The child looked slowly in the general direction of the broccoli, and then back at the man. The boy had that look on his face—the one that small children get when they have lost something they are sure will never be returned.

"Do you honestly believe," the boy said, "that that is a good reason for eating broccoli?"

From her seat between the two combatants, the mother had watched the struggle for control, the bending of childhood wills. With the boy's last remark she had, with some effort, continued to chew a mouth full of broccoli.

"It's very important," she said swallowing, "to know when to give up."

"Are you talking to me?" the two asked in union.

A small grin came across her face, revealing the slightest hint of a trapped, green vegetable.

"No...your father," the woman said, "I was talking to your father."

Miracle in the Birthing Room

She ventured slowly down that shadowed lane
Now bright with wonder and dark with pain.
The trembling thread of life stretched taut and thin
But softly then, new radiance filtered in.

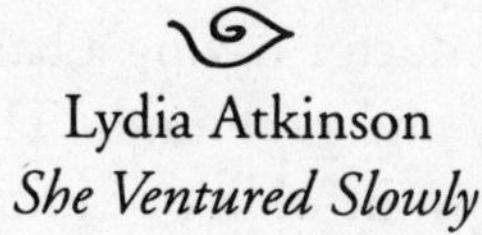

Lydia Atkinson
She Ventured Slowly

Shortly before 12:45 p.m. on a Thursday, my son Reed executed a rather nifty right-angle turn at the pelvis and successfully completed his ten-hour trip down the birth canal.

My wife did all the work, I received half the credit. When the boy pushed himself into the light, we both watched as our love miraculously multiplied, a strange and holy combination of alchemy and geometry. When the boy made his appearance, he increased by 100 percent the male population of the birthing room. Before his arrival, the room was filled with women: my wife, her doctor, and the two female nurses.

The obstetrician had been by her side for six hours. In their voices one could tell there was no place more important than my wife's bedside. For hours they talked: about children, about the demands of career and family, about men. And I got to listen.

After a few hours, one of the nurses looked at me and said, "So what do you have to say for yourself?" I began to stutter out a reply when my wife interrupted me: "Oh, don't worry about my husband; we've made him an honorary woman."

In a curious way, I was privy to what I must have been like before birth became a business and thus turned over to men. In those days, women from the neighborhood gathered to help with the birth—and to tell their stories.

In that birthing room filled with sophisticated fetal monitors and other accouterments of modern medicine, my wife was helped as much by the stories offered by her obstetrician about her own children as she was by the doctor's considerable expertise.

When the time came for pushing, encouragement came from a nurse who an hour before had told the tender tale of her son trying to run away from home when her second child was born. The obstetrician told a story on herself about the difference between a doctor delivering a baby and the doctor having a baby.

The stories were funny and profound. They were told by women engaged in what is perhaps the oldest of initiation rites. I know that there are many male obstetricians. I know that the extraordinary skill and compassion the profession demands are not easily acquired by members of either gender. But I cannot help thinking that more than anything, it was the stories of these women, so freely given, that brought forth the perseverance and courage so much needed and so readily displayed by my wife that day.

The boy has come into a world that does not always so easily understand the importance of these women's stories. It is a world where we still ask different questions of women in a confirmation hearing than we do of their male counterparts. It is a world in which personal stories told by a female physician to allay the fears of patients may be seen as unprofessional.

When the boy is old enough, I will tell him the story of how these women pitched in to give him birth. I will tell him how proud I was of his mother, how she displayed a kind of deference and attentiveness, in the midst of pain, to women who had done this many times before. I will try to give him a sense of how important these women made his mother feel, how they understood who were the two most important people in the room.

Mostly, I will tell the boy how the room into which he entered this life was full of love at the moment of his birth, and that some of that love, much of that love, was provided by women his mother hardly knew.

In each of our lives there are moments of light so clearly sacred that the illumination extends far beyond the small place where the light falls. These are, quite simply, moments of grace. The moment my son was born, he came from the womb to a sacred place. He came forth squinting at a great light.

Oh Baby, What a Smile

There are many kinds of smiles, each having a distinct character. Some announce goodness and sweetness, others betray sarcasm, bitterness and pride; some soften the countenance by their languishing tenderness, others brighten by their spiritual vivacity.

John Casper Lavater
Eighteenth-century Swiss theologian
Sermons

My infant son's first smile came at twenty-four days. An odd quizzical look came over his face like the darkness that accompanies a brewing thunderstorm.

A moment later it passed, replaced by the sun peeking out; first from the corners of his small mouth, then quickly illuminating his entire face. It animated his dull, gray baby eyes, turning them to small lakes of blue fire. It soon spread to the rest of his face, etching the first small wrinkles in his tiny brow. A moment later, the smile was gone.

The pediatrician and assorted experts on babies were skeptical about the matter. A number of older women, speaking in voices like those of TV weather forecasters predicting rain for the weekend, told me I must be mistaken.

I soon learned that there are two generally favored explanations for a baby's first smile—complete euphoria and gas. Perhaps there is no great mystery in life, save love itself, for which utter happiness and lower intestinal distress might be proffered as viable explanations.

The Spanish philosopher José Ortega y Gasset, in one of his wisest essays, points out the essential ambiguity that often accompanies human expressions and gestures. We cannot be sure, he says, why a man may raise the palms of his hands together. The man could be praying, or he might be preparing to throw himself into the sea.

Since my son's first smile, the boy has made a regular practice of it. But babies' smiles, I recently have discovered, are usually quite different from those of adults. The smile of a baby never completely disappears. Rather, it seems to dissipate, almost as if its absorbed by the eyes, returning through those windows of the soul.

The adult smile, more times than not, is accomplished entirely with facial muscles. They snap back into place after the use for the smile has passed. The adult smile too often works like a stretched rubber band. It is purely utilitarian, and can only be pulled so many times before it no longer performs its function. But the smile of a new baby is quite a different matter. It seems to have an eternal origin. It spreads like a great sea, ebbing and flowing by its own mystical tidal laws.

In Act I of *Hamlet*, Shakespeare has the melancholic Dane say that "one may smile, and smile, and be a villain." He was referring, of course, to a species of the adult smile—the studied smile, the smile of Iago and Cordelia's sisters, the half-smile of Richard Nixon telling us he is not a crook, the smile that looks for advantage before it flexes its facial muscles.

Since the birth of the boy, I have paid more attention to the nature and uses of the smile. I have come to understand that adult smiles come in many varieties: there is a kind of Cheshire cat smile, where nothing of real substance lies behind it; there are smiles of disdain and smiles of embarrassment; there are smiles of elation and smiles of profound sadness. But so few adult smiles are like those of small children.

Psychologists tell us an infant of two or three months will smile at even a half-painted dummy face if the half-countenance is equipped with two clearly defined points or circles for the eyes. More than this, the infant does not need; but he will not smile for less, for he knows that the secret to a smile is not to be found in the mouth, but rather deep within the eyes.

My small son's smiles are all of a single, holy, pedagogical piece. In these first months of life this boy has been his father's instructor. It is in its teaching function that we easily find the smile's crowning effect. Through the boy's smiles I feel recognized, perhaps even sanctified. And so, in the presence of the baby, I return his smile from deep within my eyes.

André Maurois, a twentieth-century French essayist, suggests in *The Art of Living* that we cannot completely love those at whom we cannot smile. In the past four months my son daily has shown me that Maurois is surely right. My son has taught me many things, but the most important one is this: the simplest and yet most complete form of reciprocity is to be found in the human smile.

After the Fall

Childhood: the kingdom where nobody dies.

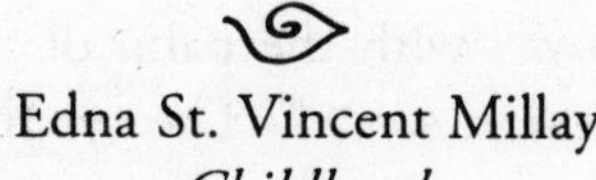

Edna St. Vincent Millay
Childhood

It happened in an instant. In the few seconds it took to wash my hands in the bathroom sink, my one-year-old son Reed had wandered out into the hall where a bag full of soiled diapers sat awaiting his attention.

A moment later, I was crawling around on my hands and knees replacing the contents of the leaking bag. I gathered up the last of the mess with one hand, and the squirming baby with the other, and headed out the front door to deposit the former and not the latter in the bin.

As I opened the door, I looked back over my shoulder to discover I had missed one. It was wedged beneath the radiator. I put the baby down by the front door, and turned to retrieve the diaper. When I turned back to face the door, Reed was gone. I rushed out to the front porch, but the baby was already in mid-flight. He had stepped off the cement porch and for the briefest of moments was flying, head down, arms and legs flailing, like a baby bird trying flight for the first or last time. Although it happened in an instant, he seemed to hang in midair, like Wile E. Coyote running off the edge of the cliff and only falling when he had realized the gravity of the situation.

In the next moment, the possibility of dread neatly had transformed itself into tragedy, and the baby lay face down at the bottom of the steps, a trickle of blood coming from beneath the left side of his face.

He did not move. The entire universe stopped: the planets sat motionless on their axes; over head, birds traveling south for the winter stopped in mid-flight; the ice in the driveway stopped melting.

I gathered him in my arms, a large wound open on his forehead, another oozing from beneath his left eye. It was only then that he began to cry, but he was still bleeding enough that I could not see the condition of the eye.

I wiped the blood away with the palm of my hand, all the time murmuring, "I'm sorry...I'm sorry." The eye had not been damaged by the fall.

I rushed the child into the house; I called my wife who was shopping. She had enough sense to dial the ambulance. It arrived in six minutes. They strapped him to a back board. He took along a stuffed animal and his father's self-recriminations.

The doctors and nurses at the hospital all possessed that strange amalgam of efficiency and compassion that makes them, like my wife, so good in a crisis. My hands shook so badly that I could not sign the forms.

I have lived what others might see as a dangerous life. I have a fairly impressive array of serious injuries and emergency surgeries to attest to this. But this was different. I have never experienced this kind of terror. In an instant, and for the first time, I understood what it must have been like to be my mother: the fluke accidents, the string of serious athletic injuries, and the dread and hope that must have always accompanied them.

Later, when I had brought the baby home, when the boy was safe and the tremors in my hands had subsided, I began to think of the children who are killed on the street every year in our city. I began to think of how a child may be on his way to school one moment and the winner of a macabre and deadly lottery the next.

Nearly every day children die on the front page of the local section of the newspaper. Before Reed's fall, I used to read about them while drinking my morning coffee. I would give the news of their deaths a little shrug, shake my head a bit, and then drive to school so I could teach my waiting students about truth, beauty, and goodness. I think I must have believed that it is natural for certain people's children to die, but certainly not mine.

Things are different now. This morning I have begun to think of the newspaper in a new way—as a place where nightmares are recorded, a ledger that calmly and dispassionately marks the loss of children, dozens of children each year in Baltimore. This morning, I have come to realize what the parents of these children must be feeling when they hear the news.

I was lucky to be awakened from my nightmare. But now I have a sense of what it is for others to live in theirs.

It must be eternal.

Wishing It Would Never End

One sits hoping in the world outside it is snowing,
hoping almost for a catastrophic deluge to add
to the romance of being in winter quarters.

Marcel Proust
Swann's Way

After the toilet paper buying frenzy. After all the milk and bread have been snatched anxiously from the shelves. After we've watched the evening weather report, nervously searching the computer-generated satellite pictures for the eye of the barometric apocalypse, like a wide-eyed man inching his chair just a little closer to a table that holds the Book of Revelation and the works of Nostradamus; after all this, it comes. And with it comes the silence.

Snow falls. It descends slowly, almost purposefully, like the tiny soap flakes gently sprinkled from the rafters above a grade school Christmas play. The snow slows all that it touches—traffic halts, schools close, my heart seems to beat by a slower, surer rhythm. This morning I want the snow to slow my life to a near standstill. I want the snow to trap the happiness in crystals, like an immortal seed trapped in blown glass.

I hold my infant son as I stare across the yard into the snow-topped evergreens at the end of the property. These trees were half this size just a few years ago. My heart is so full that a single flake might overflow it.

I want to slow time, I want this boy to remain like this, this close, his spindly legs gathered neatly in the crook of my arm, his sleeping head pressed against my slowing heart. As the boy rustles a bit, I find myself whispering, "Slow down, slow down. This moment will not last nearly long enough."

This morning, as the snow falls, I keep thinking about these ephemeral things, as if thinking about them, through some strange act of magic and desire, could make them eternal.

I begin thinking how often I have heard these same sentiments from other parents of small children and from adults who are dying. It is only from these two groups, the very young and the terminally ill, that we may learn to live entirely in the moment.

For the very young, time is an undiscovered country; for the dying, it is a means of measuring what is to be lost. The one group has not yet collected all that makes life move too quickly; the other often has cleared away much of the debris of life that too frequently gets mistaken for its essential meaning.

It is only in infants and in the very sick we seem to find the capacity to fully accept any happiness the present moment might offer. The rest of us too often reject it because in some other time, often in the distant future, it might be taken away.

Later, in the evening, I walk with the baby. The boy has inherited his father's insomnia. We move from room to room in a darkened house, his drowsy head pressed against my heart, until finally the boy gives in to the night.

In that blue snow light that filters through the window, I examine the boy. I begin to wonder if somewhere in this city under a vast blanket of winter stillness there isn't a very sick man who is awake tonight, trying, through an act of the will, to make that blue light eternal. The boy knows nothing of time, and so he sleeps. The sick man knows too much of time. I imagine him walking, and thinking, like I am, about these moments, all disappearing into the blue light.

In a few days, the snow will be gone. Schools will be open. The engine of commerce will once again assume its illusory role for all of us but the very young and the very sick. My life again will have climbed well past the posted speed limit. Living in the moment will have given way to making a living.

But right now, this baby sleeps on my chest, his breathing sharing a cadence with my beating heart, and the sick man stares out the window at the blue light, and the snow falls, gently, softly, and for the moment, it will never end.

Exchanging Dinosaurs

Necessity knows no law.

St. Augustine
On the Soul

The man was surfacing from a deep sleep. He was coming up from some strange place, perhaps his fourth grade classroom, but there were bars on the windows and it looked gray like a prison. He was about to explain to the nun why he didn't have his homework, something about the peculiar taste of the family dog for papers filled with long division, when the man fought to the surface and turned over on his other ear to discover the strange blue light of the clock radio: 5:17.

He looked back over his shoulder—the one with the rotator cuff problem—to find his sleeping wife. He thought about how she always seems less formidable when her eyes are closed. Her red hair was splayed across her faintly freckled face like a fashion model in the *New York Times Magazine* whose make-up and hair-people had spent the morning making her look that way, but she had only worn eye makeup the day they were married and when their second baby was baptized.

The man began to focus. He looked beyond his wife to discover the source of his early morning arousal. The man's seven-year-old son was standing by the side of the bed. The boy held a plastic dinosaur, a ferocious-looking thing with bright red plastic blood dripping from its jaws. The boy held the body of the dinosaur in his left hand, its disembodied right leg in the other.

"You said we could take this back today," he whispered. The boy held up the parts of the dinosaur for inspection.

"Owen, it's five o'clock in the morning. They don't even open for another five hours. Go back to bed, we'll take care of it later."

The man looked through his rear-view mirror to discover the boy's eyes, eyes the color and size of chestnuts. They were on their way to the store where they had purchased the Tyrannosaurus Rex, and the man had just informed his son that they no longer had the sales slip for the dinosaur. The boy's eyes reflected in the mirror seemed to be waiting for something, the way stranded motorists wait by the side of the highway. The boy was searching for a way to solve the dilemma, but even at his age he knew his father was the wrong place to be looking.

The man knew that the boy knew: this was his wife's department. She fixes things. She takes things back. She exchanges things. She does nearly all those unpleasant things that usually involve asking for something that one vaguely thinks is undeserved. The man has always thought of this as her job, for he understood himself as one of those people who already has enough guilt left over from childhood without the additional kind manufactured by uncooperative sales clerks.

The man's eyes moved from the mirror to the road and back again. "We can tell them it was a birthday present," the boy said to the back of his father's head. "No one ever gets a sales slip with a birthday present." The father stared at the steady brown eyes reflected in the mirror.

"Is that what you want to do?"

"Sure...otherwise I won't get my money back."

When they entered the store, the only two open cash registers were clogged with people. The boy, a few paces ahead of his father, butted in line. "Excuse me," the boy said, but before he could finish his sentence the check-out clerk saw the dinosaur box. With eyes fixed on the black conveyor built rolling toward her, she pointed with her right arm toward the back of the store.

"You'll have to see the manager."

The manager was a small woman with black bifocals and a curly yellow necklace full of store keys. Her office was a small cubicle full of empty clothes hangers. She saw the boy coming.

"I know...I know...it's the right leg, the whole lot was like that. Take another one from that pile over there. Leave the broken one here."

For a moment the boy did not move, then, very quickly he followed the woman's instructions. He acted like a prisoner might who accidentally had just been given his freedom. By the time he returned to the car, the boy already had checked the condition of the new dinosaur's legs. As the man settled into the driver seat, he gave a quick glance back at the boy taking inventory of the Tyrannosaurus's plastic parts. The man started the car and adjusted the mirror . He watched the image of the boy examining the contents of the new box. Shrink-wrap and fragments of discarded cardboard littered the back seat. Without looking up, the boy could feel his father's eyes on him.

"I know what you're going to tell me...you're going to say something about how I didn't have to tell the lie and it worked out okay anyway...you're going to tell me that it is always right to tell the truth."

He looked up to meet his father's eyes in the mirror. "But I hope you are not going to tell me that every time you don't tell the lie things work out for the best... because... Dad...that would be a lie."

That evening the man thought a lot about what the boy had said. He thought about how, when he was the boy's age, it was very clear to him that lies are always wrong. He thought about how most of us tell our children the same thing—that there is an invisible, odorless, and tasteless rule about always telling the truth. The rule hovers just above us somewhere. When the man was seven he thought that this rule about truth-telling lived with a bunch of other similar rules somewhere just above the clouds.

The man also thought about that Christmas song:

He knows when you are sleeping
and he knows when you're awake.
He knows when you've been bad or good,
so be good for goodness sake.

For the month before Christmas, he always sang this song to his children—just as it had been sung to him. But now, for the first time, he wondered what the last line meant. "So be good for goodness sake." Was it an exclamation: for goodness sake! Or was the song telling us to be good simply for the sake of being good? And he wondered why, even as an adult, he had never noticed the ambiguity of the final line.

Later in the evening, the man had another dream. He dreamt that the boy had fallen from a cloud, and that red fire trucks and emergency vehicles lined a large green field where it was believed the boy would come down. Somehow the man knew it was his responsibility to catch the falling boy.

For hours they waited: fire fighters, paramedics, police officers, all with their radios crackling. And the father waited, while invisible cicada waited too for the people to all go home The father waited, he waited in the middle of the field, callused hands outstretched, his eyes squinting at the sky.

The man's arms and eyes became tired, but still he waited. Suddenly the boy burst forth from a swirling mass of gray and white clouds, his arms and legs flailing out of control like a baby bird trying flight for the first time. Minicams caught the entire flight, but the father awakened before the boy hit the ground.

A Rag Bag Hung on its Nail

Works of art can wait: indeed, they do nothing but that and do it passionately.

Rainer Maria Rilke
Letters of Rainer Maria Rilke
1892-1910

Works of art are of an infinite loneliness and with nothing so little to be reached as with criticism. Only love can grasp and hold and fairly judge them.

Rainer Maria Rilke
Letters to a Young Poet

We spent the Thanksgiving holiday in the Appalachian Mountains, my wife and I, and our two small boys—far from the city and the complexities of holiday family life. We came to a cabin in the West Virginia panhandle to escape twenty pound turkeys, gravy boats filled to the brim, and too many television reports of guilt-ridden middle class people volunteering for the day at soup kitchens and homeless shelters all over town.

We walked along a mountain path at dusk. The sky in the west had turned magenta against the backdrop of the mountains, smoke rose from woodstoves in cabins all along the ridge.

In his autobiography, Henry James calls memory "a rag bag hung on its nail in the closet." One could write for decades and never produce a metaphor as clear and as true. Indeed, if the essayist has an appointed task (perhaps "calling" would be a better word), it is to ceaselessly examine the contents of the rag bag, never letting it settle for too long on its nail.

E.B. White, in one of his most evocative essays, "The Ring of Time," says something of the *raison d'être* of the essayist. He talks of feeling charged with the safe-keeping of all "unexpected items of worldly and unworldly enchantment." He writes of feeling held personally responsible if even the smallest experience and its concomitant memory were ever to be lost.

As White moved into old age, it is quite clear from his essays, that the transitory, the ephemeral, became for him wholly identified with the beautiful. As I move more deeply into middle age, I more and more agree. And if White is correct that the transitory and the beautiful are so often inextricably bound together, then it became just as clear to me as I walked with my family along that mountain road, in all the twilight that was left to us, that a certain kind of memory is nothing more than a ubiquitous but perhaps little understood species of love—a love so deeply felt that it alone can account for the human heart's tendency to a mixture of euphoria and melancholy when trying to recapture the goodness and the beauty of the past.

Walking along the mountain path this evening, as the last of the pale purple light was gathering just on the other side of the mountains, and the scent of the woodstoves drifted across a valley full of trees stripped to their winter essentials, suddenly I found myself transported, standing in the woods with my father on a cold November evening in 1954. We were outside a small log cabin my uncle owned somewhere in the Pennsylvania mountains.

One memory led quickly to another until time evaporated, like the thin wisps of smoke dissipating on the horizon. All that remained were the silent stars, the smell of wood fires, and the rough feel of my father's calluses wrapped around the dimpled four-year-old fingers of my right hand. I held his hand tightly and made a series of wishes, all now long forgotten.

I cannot remember much else about that Pennsylvania cabin. I can recall sleeping wrapped up in army blankets with my twin sisters on the cabin floor. I remember thinking how much my sisters were like a perfectly matched pair of shoes, and how each would be useless without the other. But mostly I recall how much I loved and needed them both as big sisters.

Later in the evening, while sitting alone by the woodstove in the West Virginia cabin, it occurs to me that I have not thought about my uncle's cabin, nor about my sisters as an inseparable pair, for nearly forty years. A moment later, I begin thinking about my younger son who spent the morning riding in a frame pack on my back. Along with his mother and his older brother we walked a few hills, crossed a log bridge, and hiked around a small lake that glistened in the sunlight.

Forty years from now the boy will be just a bit younger than I am now. If I am still among the living, I will be a few weeks shy of my eighty-fourth birthday. As I stare into the fire of the woodstove, I begin to wonder if my son will recall this day: the sight of his mother standing by the lake, oblivious as usual to her great beauty; his older brother doing all the right things, as my sisters always did; and his father's whispered love.

If he does recall this holiday, it will be love that was the keeper of memory, as rich and as secret as buried treasure. And it is love that will bring back this day, as clear and as bright as the sun dancing on the surface of a tiny lake in the middle of the West Virginia woods.

Chapter

Seven

On Reading, Writing, and Teaching

By reading, we enjoy the dead; by teaching, the living; and by writing, ourselves. Reading enriches the memory; teaching, the wit; and writing, the judgment. Of these, reading is by far the most important, for it furnishes us with both the others.

Caleb Colton

By even the most conservative of estimates, I spend more than two-thirds of my time reading, writing, and teaching. Along with husbandry and fatherhood, these are not simply the things I do, they are who I am. Most of the essays in this chapter speak for themselves. I hope they convey something of the reverence I have for my colleagues, past and present, for my students, and above all, for the written word.

The Effacing of Memory

Memory is not just the imprint of the past upon us;
it is the keeper of what is meaningful for our deepest hopes and fears.

Rollo May
Man's Search for Himself

Deep in the minds of all but the barely sentient of us there exists an omnipresent tension, a small but important battle waged in the recesses of neurons and synapses. It is a struggle between longing to remember and a tendency, or perhaps some would say a need, to forget. Some are blessed, or perhaps cursed, with total recall, while others find it difficult to remember even the most poignant of moments.

It is usually difficult to decide with any real certainty whether there is such a thing as unintentional forgetting. Psychologists and philosophers since Plato have debated the matter with no definitive conclusion. Nevertheless, it is safe to say that one of the best measures of an individual, or an entire culture for that matter, is what he, she, or it remembers, and what remains buried and forgotten.

Loren Eiseley, the poet-anthropologist, in one of his finest essays discusses the rather bizarre case in which he was called in to help in the identification of a suicide victim who had so carefully effaced all his individuating characteristics that it was impossible for the experts to say with any certitude who the man had been. The *rigor mortal* stranger was a real life (death) example of what Martin Smith had created in his *Gorky Park*, except here Eiseley's dead man was responsible for his own anonymity. His body stood as a macabre work of art. The unknown sculptor had made oblivion his artistic goal.

One element in the telling of history that continues to fascinate me is how sometimes entire cultures, or at least large portions of them, set out, intentionally or not, to practice the art of Eiseley's dead stranger. The tombs and monuments of Iknaten, the Egyptian founder of solar monotheism, were defaced and rendered anonymous shortly after his death. The ancient city of Carthage appears to have suffered a similar fate at the hands of the invading Romans. The makers of the French revolution in the late eighteenth century attempted to destroy the Christian calendar and thus eliminate the last vestiges of a bourgeois and corrupt Christian morality. In our own time, each succeeding edition of the *Soviet Encyclopedia* graphically illustrated the point that sometimes entire cultures knowingly and painstakingly forget.

In the past few years I have become increasingly more concerned that we in this country are on the verge of a similar process of amnesia. I do not know whether it is the intentional kind of forgetting like that practiced by Eiseley's dead stranger and the editors of the *Soviet Encyclopedia*, or if it is a more unconscious process of *damnatio memoriae*, lost memory. What is clear is that it is the kind of forgetting that occurs slowly, over time, like the gradual washing away of finely constructed sand castles on the beach: first form is obliterated, followed by substance.

In this country we have forgotten the languages spoken by our grandparents, and we seem to have no real desire to relearn them. Across the country language requirements have been reduced or eliminated in a good many high schools, as well as some of our best colleges and universities.

We also no longer read. In the past fifteen years we have witnessed the selling or dismantling of several of this nation's greatest newspapers. Melville's classic novel *Moby Dick* is read by local high school students in an edition "for the modern reader." This helpful edition not only eliminates much of Melville's "difficult prose," but it also excises all the whaling chapters, including "The Whiteness of the Whale," the very heart of the book.

For many of us those stretches of silence where one could sit with a good book and be transported to another world, a better world, by virtue of another's literary craft and the strength of one's own imagination, have been replaced by large obtrusive boxes that provide an endless series of mass produced daydreams designed to allow us to avoid thinking too deeply or too clearly about anything.

We have traded Don Quixote and Sancho Panchez for Oprah and Geraldo. We have eliminated Othello in favor of scenes from the O.J. trial. Along the way, we have forgotten a great deal: geography, history, how to write and speak, and how to behave in public.

Many of us are hoodwinked these days in believing that technological advancement and wisdom are synonymous. We no longer understand, as all great cultures have, that science confers power, not purpose. Technology has promised us two things that are not always connected: power and wisdom. It only regularly keeps the first promise. This is because of the worst case of our forgetting, we have forgotten what wisdom is.

Finding Other Voices

How wonderful is the human voice.
It is the organ of the soul.

Henry Wadsworth Longfellow

Editing is not an easy job, especially for daily newspaper editors. The job description should read something like:

> WANTED: editor with a reverence for the written word, and the sense and grace to say "yes" to the right pieces, and the courage and gentleness to say "no" to the wrong ones. Applicants must have thick skin, somewhat repressed poetic sensibilities, and an eye for the smallest of details. He or she must be able and willing to deal with some folks who can't write, while fervently believing they can, and, more importantly, with those who are not so sure they can write, but with a little hand-holding and gentle ego-massaging just might produce something that later will be fastened with fruit-shaped magnets to the fronts of refrigerators all over Pig Town and Pennsylvania Avenue, and Govans to Guilford. The patience of Job and the judgment of Solomon would be helpful, though not required.

Since March, 1979, first Gwinn Owens and then Mike Bowler have routinely performed these difficult tasks for the *Evening Sun's* "Other Voices" page: selecting and editing twenty pieces a week, eighty a month, 960 a year, 14,640 in all, with periodic time off for good behavior. Those 14,640 essays, poems, and reviews were culled from 72,000 submissions, most of which can still be found in the "Other Voices" editor's somewhat cluttered office.

Some of the winners came from an eloquent aluminum siding salesman, with a love of the Orioles and a taste for whimsy; from academics of all flavors; and, in the early years, from an electrician, a high school graduate who, when the spirit moved him, happened to write like James Joyce. His poetic and sometimes fierce submissions were always hastily typed on stationery that included his home improvement license number in the upper right corner.

If I have learned anything in reading this special page for the last fifteen years, it is that good writing, like love, flashes in a moment of moments, and flows when and where it will. Beautiful prose is like wild flowers, there is no telling where you might find them. We might expect an elegant poem from a Carmelite nun in Towson or a lyrical piece on the changing of the seasons from local priest/poet. Perhaps there will appear a pristine essay from a writing teacher in Timonium or a clear and cogent article on Lincoln by a local history teacher who also happens to be a successful high school football coach. These pieces came to this page as no great surprises. But then there are the others: mothers writing from kitchen tables in Arbutus; a cab driver with a keen sense of character and a flair for the subordinate clause; an inmate poet and playwright who tells us more about violence and freedom than it is comfortable for most of us to hear; and a former homeless woman who writes about what happens when the oppressed become racists themselves.

"Other Voices" always has had room for people with something on their minds or those who wish to get something off their chests. But it also has featured some flat-out good writing: prose and poetry from those who might otherwise have never experienced the delight of seeing their own byline.

For the past few years these "other voices," along with Gilbert Sandler and the few remaining columnists on board, have been what has kept the *Evening Sun* from becoming the final edition of the morning paper, or, still worse, the daily paper delivered in a Potempkin village. Alas, the *Evening Sun* is sinking beyond the horizon.

When Mike Bowler stepped down as the editor of this page, we lost a cigar-smoking anomaly: a man who knows that language is a solemn thing, something that grows out of a reflective life—out of the agonies and ecstasies, its wants and its weariness. He was a thoughtful editor, a man long on local issues and short on pretense. One cannot think about Mike Bowler's exit from that cramped little editor's office, with out also thinking about the end of a newspaper era—a time when a bottle of white out and a bottle of bourbon could be found in most reporters' top desk drawer.

If you have ever written for the "Other Voices" page, you might from time to time lift a glass of beer to Bowler, Owens, and other editors like them. Perhaps the only real task of a good editor—one embodied in the job description found above—is to know a good writer when you see one. For the past fifteen years, they have seen a lot of them, and then put them on the "Other Voices" page for the rest of us to see.

Henry James, in his autobiography *Middle Years*, aptly describes those of us who try regularly to put pen to paper, or fingers to word-processor keys: "We work in the dark, we do what we can. We give what we have. Our doubt is our passion, and our passion is our task. The rest is the madness of art."

Thank you editors for bringing our madness to light. Cheers!

The Sinking of the *Evening Sun*

There is an elegance in the morning and in the evening suns. But the evening sun is more beautiful because its departure is like a lament.

Tacitus

Like a nervous relative pacing the hospital waiting room, I look for things to occupy my time—something to suggest a miracle is in the offing and the dearly beloved's parting can somehow be postponed. Barring a miracle, I would be willing to settle for something to reaffirm the critically ill loved one's worth. It is not so easy when it is a newspaper, the *Evening Sun*, that is doing the dying.

I have written for the *Evening Sun* and its "Other Voices" page for a number of years. I have grown to love this paper the way one becomes attached to a quirky uncle, one who has gravy stains on his tie, but never seems to run out of good stories.

We will soon be a one newspaper town for the first time since the early nineteenth century. It happened through a curious act of suicide, or perhaps it was homicide cleverly made to look like a self-inflicted wound. What I do know is that the switchboard operator now answers the phone with the conspicuously singular, "Baltimore Sunpaper." The circulation department recently conducted a contest to see which employee could convert the most number of evening subscribers to the morning paper. The evening paper is no longer sold in vending machines on the eastern shore of Maryland and Delaware.

If you question the value of having more than one daily newspaper, consider the two papers' treatments of a couple of news items: the confirmation hearings of Clarence Thomas and the death of former police commissioner William Pommerleau. Both stories came before the consolidation of the two editorial staffs.

The morning paper heartily endorsed Mr. Thomas, both before and after the hearings, while the *Evening Sun* suggested before the hearings that Clarence Thomas was not suitable for the highest court in the land. In an excellent editorial after the hearings, the evening paper simply reiterated their earlier view.

After the former police commissioner's death, *The Sun* editorial page talked about Mr. Pommerleau's accomplishments with a fawning deference, while the evening paper, in a much more evenhanded editorial, pointed out the commissioner's many weaknesses along with his accomplishments.

Now the *Evening Sun* is sinking. And when it is finally gone, it may well make history. Not just because the paper of H.L. Mencken will be dead, but also because it will be the first time in nautical history when a proud ship manages to abandon its sinking rats.

(The final edition of the *Evening Sun* rolled off the presses on September 15, 1995.)

Letters

An intention to write never turns into a letter. A letter must happen to one, to sender and receiver, like a surprise.

Rainer Maria Rilke
Letters 1892-1910

There is an old wooden box with a silver clasp and red velvet innards that rests in the bottom right drawer of my writing desk. Inside are a few dozen letters from a lost love, a woman I have not seen in nearly a decade. Everything else that once connected my life to hers is gone, but the letters remain in the drawer, close enough that they provide a bittersweet kind of comfort, yet far enough away that they rarely become the object of any sustained reverie.

I don't know what it is about old love letters that makes them so difficult to give up. The pictures are gone, and I no longer remember her phone number. I don't know what kind of car she now drives, nor whether she still eats poppy bagels for breakfast. But I have kept her letters, and sometimes, while my wife and two small boys are sleeping, I tip-toe into my study and reread a few of them. I examine the handwriting for clues, the way an Egyptologist must pore over the curve of every hieroglyph. Sometimes I allow myself to wonder if she has kept my letters as well.

It is not only love letters we keep: there are the other special ones, the letters that tie us ineluctably to both the living and the dead. There are the letters that say goodbye for good and the ones that say goodbye forever. And there are the letters that have convinced us, often at precisely the right time, that we are better than we really are. We always keep those letters that in a moment's reading secretly and silently have made us the people we have become.

There is a special kind of power that only these letters possess. We carry them around in books and coat pockets. We hide them away in desk drawers . We reread them in stolen moments. The return address acts as proof positive that the rest of the world is not simply the dream of a lonely solipsist. The right kind of letter reminds us that there is someone out there who knows where and why we live.

It is perhaps the best measure of the complicated economy of our affections to examine our feelings when first discovering the identity of the sender of a letter. There is a fine sense of anticipation that only comes upon the discovery of certain return addresses. These days purveyors of junk mail play on this sense of anticipation by dressing up their missives to look like something that might have been sent from the Internal Revenue Service.

Ann Morrow Lindbergh in *Bring Me a Unicorn* suggests that people are often most fully real as letter writers, for the writer becomes a focused spirit, while in face to face conversation the heaviness of matter is often too much in evidence. Sometimes the very body of a person is an impediment to any genuine encounter. Some special communications sorely need the sacred space and silence that only letters provide. This is why the telephone so often will not do on these occasions.

Despite our obvious need for these small brushes with the eternal, few of us write real letters anymore. My maternal grandmother accomplished in a week of letter writing what I now manage in a year: individual letters to each of her six children; missives to the grocer, the cobbler, and butcher; thank you notes for favors large and small; and to a recalcitrant grandson a rather long letter on the finer points of

English grammar that begins: "You must always remember, chickens are 'done,' while human beings are 'finished.'"

When we do receive letters these days, they sometimes come from a fax machine. It is hard to imagine a love letter coming from a fax machine, but now I suppose they do. The machine must beep and whir as it always does, and then out comes the love letter without a jacket on. Love letters, of course, should never reveal nor hide too much, so a faxed love letter begins with a decided disadvantage: it comes without an envelope.

I wonder if sometime soon no one will write letters. Perhaps we will simply send our thoughts around for everyone to see on machines that go beep and whir. We will propose marriage, ask for forgiveness, and mourn for our dead on faxes and Internet, and no one's thoughts will ever wear a jacket again.

A dear friend of mine once defined an incurable optimist as one who checks the mail box on Sunday. I worry that someday soon our trips to the mailbox will all be Sundays. For letters are, by their very nature, products of disembodied souls. And the giving and receiving of letters is as close as many come to a life of the spirit.

Learning Lessons

The moralist ought not simply to draw from his own when attempting to paint the minds of others.

J. Petit-Senn
Conceits and Caprices

Recently, through a series of inexplicable and equally improbably events, I was named the Carnegie Foundation's "Maryland Professor of the Year." I don't know how it happened. The process had all the drama and suspense, and about the same amount of predictability, as a man being struck by lightning.

A few weeks before the announcement was made public, the folks from Carnegie called to give me the news. At first I felt like one of those poor souls on the "Queen for a Day" television show. You remember the ones. The audience felt so sorry for them that they gave them new refrigerators and vacuum cleaners. But soon the tone of that first phone conversation changed dramatically. I was told that as a part of the festivities I was to teach philosophy for three hours to various groups of seventh graders at a middle school in center-city Washington. Distinguished members of the press and the academic community would be invited to witness the whole thing. It was not immediately clear to me what the people who didn't win would be required to do. Perhaps jump off the Washington Monument, I didn't ask.

After spending the morning at the middle school, the seven anointed professors of the year were to be escorted around the city, eventually making our way to the *USA Today* building in northern Virginia, where we would be feted and praised by newspaper moguls, politicians, and academic luminaries, large and small.

In one of his finest essays, Loren Eiseley talks about finding good teachers in the oddest of places. Although I was prepared to find superior teaching going on at the middle school, I was not ready for the fact that my teacher would be a twelve-year-old boy named Lionel.

Before going to Washington, I had decided to tell the children a part of the story of Huck Finn. In this short section of the novel, Huck has helped Jim, a slave, to escape his owner, Miss Watson. Huck and Jim find themselves floating on the Mississippi on a raft. With each bend in the river, the pair comes closer to Cairo, Illinois, where Jim will become a free man.

Along the way, Jim thanks Huck effusively for helping him escape. But Huck begins to feel guilty, for he knows that helping Jim was as good as stealing. Huck tells Jim he is going to leave the raft on a small canoe, so that he might scout out to see if it is safe for Jim to go ashore. While paddling to the riverbank, however, it is clear that Huck plans to turn Jim in.

On the way, Jim is accosted by two men with hound dogs and shotguns. These bounty hunters are looking for escaped slaves. The day is misty, and the white men look out at the raft. They ask Huck a simple question: "That man on the raft, is he white or black?" For a moment Huck hesitates; finally, he says, "white man."

I told these children this story because Huck was about their age, and I wanted them to think about the difficulty of knowing and doing the good. I wanted them to know that sometimes there is a harrowing ambiguity that accompanies moral decision making, but I was a little worried that the subtlety of Huck's dilemma might not be so easily grasped. I thought they would naturally be interested in the story, but I was not aware that one of them, Lionel, would be my teacher.

When I finished telling them Huck and Jim's tale, I waited for a response. For a moment no one said a word. Then Lionel raised his hand. He was a short boy with skin a deep, rich brown color. "I think this story is about my life, " the boy said. I smiled a bit.

"How's that?" I finally said.

"Well, Huck had to tell a lie to save a black man's life," he said. "Last week, I saw a man shot on 14th Street and when the police came and asked around if anybody seen anything, I said 'I was tying my shoes. I didn't see nothing.' The way I figure it, I had to tell a lie to save a black man's life—my own."

At first I was confused, the way one sitting in a train station is often mistaken, when the train starts off, about the platform moving. A moment later I was wondering what I was doing at an inner-city middle school trying to teach these children about moral ambiguity.

In the evening, amidst a good bit of fanfare, I received my award.

Why Most of My Friends are Nuns Over Seventy

I believe that one has to be seventy before one is full of courage. The young are always half-hearted.

D.H. Lawrence
Letters

For fifteen years I have been hopelessly in love with another woman. My wife and I talk about it all the time. My spouse is very broad-minded about it, she even encourages me to pursue this other relationship. I think she understands that this kind of love doesn't come along very often, for there are very few love affairs these days that might properly be called Platonic. I am lucky enough to be involved in one with an eighty-year-old nun.

Sister Virgina. When I first saw the name I thought it was a misprint; next it brought to mind a Mediterranean-looking middle-aged woman, with lots of costume jewelry, and an open-palmed, red neon sign blinking enticingly from her front yard: Sister Virgina—Reader and Advisor. Then I figured she must have been named after one of those female saints in St. Augustine's *City of God*—the ones who dived off tall buildings to avoid being sullied by the Vandals and Goths as they brought a premature end to the Roman Empire.

I was not ready for Sister Virgina. She was so gentle looking: barely 100 pounds, but with sturdy little legs, and eyes that twinkle when she laughed. I came for a job interview. I thought she would ask me tough questions about Plato and Aristotle. Instead she wanted to know if I had eaten any lunch yet.

I took the job. In that first year Sister Virgina asked me to write a letter in support of her application for a sabbatical. I remember inquiring about how long it had been since her last leave. She had not had one in her first forty-three years of teaching. A week later, when I handed her the letter, I told her I was giving it to her with one important string attached: she could not bother me again about the sabbatical nonsense for another forty-three years. After agreeing that she would not bother me about such egregiously special treatment for another forty-three years, we sealed the deal. She never did take the leave. Now she has been teaching for fifty-eight years. I think she really believes she can't ask me for another letter in her behalf for twenty-eight years. I will only be mildly surprised if she is around then, still teaching.

When she was a younger nun, Sister Virgina taught from September to June. Then, in black habit with starched white veil, she instructed the order's novices for eight weeks of summer school. In August, she received her compensation for the summer's labors: a $5 mass card on which she was permitted to inscribe the name of the recipient. It was thought by the powers that be that it was a bit too self-indulgent to scribble one's own name on the card, though surely she could have used the grace by the end of a typical Baltimore summer before air-conditioning.

I am not sure why I love this woman so much. Maybe it is simply that she is the only other person I know who loses her keys fortnightly. She almost always finds them in the same place. Even this seems like a metaphor for her dependability. Perhaps my love for Sister Virgina has come from watching her year after year give away the royalties on her books to the college's scholarship fund. Or maybe it is because I have not seen her display anger in fifteen years of watching closely. For Sister Virgina, goodness is a vivid and pristine thing, as clear as crystal, as unmistakable as the smell of cinnamon. For most people, even the really good among us, God is a belief. To Sister Virgina, He is an embrace. That is why for the past fifteen years I have been playing a kind of spiritual Harold to her metaphysical Maude.

A few years ago Sister Virgina had major surgery. I bit my fingernails while sitting with her flesh-and-blood sister in the waiting room. Later, I heard through the religious grapevine that a few of the other nuns were a bit uncomfortable with the intimacy this implied. But I could not think of anything else but the surgery. I could not be anywhere else but the waiting room.

Looking back, the possibility of losing Sister Virgina gave birth in me to a kind of longing I don't think I had had before that day. The same feeling of longing is tied to the strong desire for immortality, not for myself, but for this woman who seems so much like goodness itself.

I have had this same longing just recently whenever I think of another colleague, a nearly blind octogenarian Milton scholar. She is trying to set the record straight on one of our college's founders. She works on her project every day. She works through various nagging pains brought to her by eight and a half decades of walking upright on the planet. She is a constant reminder of the nature and purposes of courage. For six decades she has quietly prepared her place in a long line of blind seers, stretching back to Homer and his Tiresias, through Galileo, and on to Milton and his Samson.

A third sister, a recently retired English professor, is a poet filled with such grace and a moral beauty of so rare a kind that the longing comes as well whenever my thoughts turn to her absence from the classroom. These women should have their faces carved on someone's Mount Rushmore. There should be some kind of award for having the needle of one's moral compass point perpetually north. I can't imagine anyone, even forty years from now, wanting to enshrine my generation's sense of the moral good. It would be an embarrassment, like someone replacing the presidents' faces with a series of Alfred E.

Newmans set in stone.

More and more these days when I think of my generation's moral sensibilities I am reminded of those hapless pilots in certain equatorial waters who find their compasses spinning violently, erratically, incapable of finding true north. So many forty-somethings are on the fast track, but it is not clear where we are going. It is as if we have not stopped to think that after we win the rat race, we will still be rats.

Sometimes I think of my generation as traveling in progressively wider concentric circles, forever turning away from the center, while all the time convincing each other that the scenery is changing and that we are almost there. We are not so much rudderless, as we are possessors of a collective bad sense of direction, a kind of malady that leaves us profoundly, perhaps tragically, incapable of knowing which way to go.

My generation is uncomfortable with categories like sin, grace, and redemption, so we turn the former into a progressively more tiresome litany about addiction and co-dependence, forfeiting the very concept of responsibility we so ardently believe we are fostering in our usually over-indulged children.

We forty-somethings grew to adulthood—or at least to what passes these days for adulthood—with something called "values clarification," a 1960s and early 70s form of relativism that masqueraded as a substitute for a substantive moral education. We were left with the impression that Charles Manson's values were just as good as Mother Teresa's, it was just a matter of getting them clarified.

Mine is a generation where the practice of individual and collective redacted history has been honed to something near perfection. No one but the hapless Judge Ginsberg and myself seem to have smoked marijuana in college. We spoke then with a special fervor about helping others, and now, as we close in on middle age, we elect our peers at midterm national elections, so that they can return charity to the private sector where it belongs. At the same time, we forty-somethings give proportionally less to organized charities than any other adult cohort, save the X-generation.

We were the first generation to blame everything on our parents.

Now we want to make sure we hold criminals and welfare recipients responsible for their behavior, while continuing to feed a post-Cold War defense budget that has yet to be significantly reduced.

We are a collection of Barney Fifes taking over for the recently retired Andy. We are all Lucy Ricardos, with crooked paste-on mustaches, disguised as waiters at the Copa Cabana. We are all the more nervous now that one of us has become the head waiter.

On the edge of campus there is a tiny cemetery. It is filled with the bones and simple grave markers of a few dozen strong and courageous women who have come before Sister Virgina and my two other friends. Most of these nuns are finally enjoying their first sabbaticals. Someday my friends will be placed alongside their sisters. It is there they will wait patiently for the resurrection. Anyone who knows them is fairly certain about their destination.

But I must confess: I remain uncertain about where my generation is headed.

On Why I Teach

Benevolence alone will not make a teacher, nor will learning alone do it. The gift of teaching is a peculiar talent, and implies a need and a craving in the teacher himself.

John Jay Chapman
Memories and Milestones

I have just found the form for the Carnegie Teaching Awards among a pile of half-graded term papers. Several dozen overdue library books grace the other side of my desk. I have a pile of unreturned phone messages on my desk chair, and the annual report of my academic achievements, as well as my departmental review, are due in the morning. These forms are giving my paper weight a reason for being on the window sill behind my desk. Outside my window on the fourth floor, stately oaks, trees older than this proud and century-old college, majestically stand. I have come to the end of my twenty-first year of teaching. In that time I have taught about 8,000 undergraduates. And now I have the daunting task of writing a three page essay about my teaching.

I was not a very good student until I got to college. A handful of fine undergraduate teachers coaxed and pulled what they suspected might be a scholar cleverly hidden somewhere in my soul. As an undergraduate, I was constantly shown models of good teaching. If I learned anything from these examples, it is that fine teaching, though rare, may come in many shapes and sizes.

What I try to do, in and out of my classroom, is listen as much as I speak. I have my students sit in a circle, so that no one can hide, and people know when someone is missing. I explain at the outset of a class that we need every mind in the room to deal with the philosophical issues at hand.

I believe there are philosophical passions to be found in nearly every student. I think of my job not so much as a person who instills passion, as one who finds it. Sometimes I find it in the oddest of places. This is why I continue to teach. Around the next bend, in that next class, or during my next office hours, someone may walk into my life and, with her passion and intelligence, change the both of us forever. My teaching career has lived on examples, so permit me to talk about one to give you some sense of what it is I do.

Four years ago a young homeless woman walked into my office. She had been given a full scholarship to the college, and, after a few false starts in the business and communication arts departments, she told me, quite unapologetically, that she wished to be a professor of medieval philosophy. For the next seven semesters, we worked together: learning philosophy, studying Latin grammar, and acquiring habits of thought that might translate into a lasting life of the mind.

During the same time, my student, using an extraordinary sense of humor and keeping her eye fixed unblinkingly on her goal, fought a list of setbacks and indignities that, like the violence in Greek tragedy, is best left off-stage.

When it came time to applying for graduate school, I told the woman that she should go for broke. Among her choices were the divinity schools at Harvard, Yale, and the University of Chicago. The most important of my undergraduate teachers had urged me to do the same twenty-three years ago. When I arrived at Yale, I kept wondering when they would discover their mistake. I used to have a recurring dream that the Dean of Students would knock on the door one day to tell me firmly but politely that someone in New Jersey who had a name very similar to mine had accidentally been sent my rejection notice, and could I leave now because he is out in the hallway with his stuff, waiting to move in.

I know my student feels the same way, but she will attend the University of Chicago, where she has accepted one of the largest stipends ever given by the University for graduate study. She plans to study medieval philosophy.

So that's what I do. I find intelligent, passionate people, and then I try to convince them that they can do amazing things. Usually they do, and then, somehow, I manage to get much of the credit.

Someday my student will be sitting in her faculty office and a student will walk in and change her life forever. She will tell the student her story. That student will go on to do amazing things. They will give my student most of the credit for it. Then, my student will call me and tell me about it, and we both will laugh.

A Teacher's Talisman

I have sometimes wondered whether my pupils realize the intensity of feeling which underlay a decorous classroom manner of dealing with certain books and writers. Perhaps I give myself away when I read poetry aloud.

Bliss Perry
And Gladly Teach

Those of us who teach consider the year to begin in early September and to drag on, sometimes interminably, to the beginning of June. The rest of the year is recuperation.

No other job could dispossess and incapacitate one so completely as teaching. You could work all year in a toll booth or on an assembly line, you could work as a bank teller or change flat tires, and at the end of the year you would still pretty much remain the same person. For teachers there is no chance.

Teaching annually obliterates all who do it well. It cuts right into one's very being. It takes over the spirit. It drags the real "you" out of the most clever hiding places and displays it before some of the best and worst critics on Earth.

Among those critics are some who are not ready to be taught. These students did not buy their books at the beginning of the term and wonder impatiently about the secrets to be found there later in the semester. They close their notebooks and texts five minutes before the end of class. They practice the most intricate forms of out-of-body experiences, while pushing a well-chewed pencil across a soon to be discarded notebook. These days I see too many students who are not ready to learn. They see me and my work as irrelevant, an annoyance to be climbed over or walked around on the way to wherever they think they are going.

These students usually see their education as a series of inoculations, in which they grudgingly submit to painful shots of history, philosophy, or literature, so they don't come down with a serious case later on. These students don't read newspapers, they don't go to plays or museums, and they have never been to a classical concert.

I see these students walk across the stage at graduation and I know I have failed them. They wave their diplomas over their heads as though they are talismans warding off ignorance. They have become official possessors of knowledge and they come to believe that since they have an epistemological union card, society will find them the proper job.

Fortunately, there are other stories to tell from my classroom. These stories have many plots and an ever-changing cast of characters, but one constant theme is courage—like that found in one of my former students, a homeless woman who overcame the odds and earned a scholarship to a prestigious university.

Her story, in particular, is a dramatic tale. I could tell you others. They don't all glow in the dark like this one, but they possess the same kind of uncanny courage. There is the straight-A student with three growing boys and a disabled daughter. She always completes her assignments and asks wonderful questions in and out of class. There is the twenty-one-year-old graduating senior who will be married in a few days to a military man. A few days later he will fly to Korea, without her, for two years. She spent the spring acting in a Shakespeare play, working on an independent study project, editing a book for a faculty member, and worrying about the future, while making "A"s.

Indeed, if twenty years of teaching has, in turn, taught me anything, I have learned that the highest forms of courage are the mundane varieties, for they are constant and character forming. These silent kinds of courage endure. One of the major reasons I will return to the classroom in the fall is because of these smaller brands of heroism. I secretly carry them around with me.

For the summer, they are my talismans.

Little Deaths and Tiny Resurrections

Going away I can generally bear the separation, but I don't like the leave-taking.

Samuel Butler
Letters

The life of a teacher is so often a curious affair. We seem always to be doing things backwards, while much of the rest of the world is intent on going the right way. We call our graduation ceremonies "commencements," rather than the denouements that they clearly are. We bring an end to things academic at precisely that time of year when nearly all of the natural world is shouting that things are just beginning. We begin again in the fall, when the world of nature is winding down its biological clock. We also experience those tiny deaths and resurrections, those rehearsals for the end, that only come with this very serious business of teaching. But while teachers are thinking of the end, our graduating students see themselves as embarking on the beginning, a rebirth into a new life.

Every May, my graduating students have a series of goodbyes to make. They get to prepare for them for four years. It is painful for them to say farewell to favorite teachers and trusted friends, to favorite trees and favorite classes, and yet they do it, bolstered by the excitement of a movement into what they still insist on calling "the real world."

Teachers have to say goodbye every year. We never get to prepare. There is rarely time for anticipatory grief. After wrestling with term papers and exams for several days, we wake up one morning in the end of May, we don our preposterous looking robes and mortar boards, and say farewell to people with whom we have shared the very ideas that make us the people we have chosen to become. After the ceremony we walk around in our Medieval monks robes and hug perfect strangers because they have entrusted family members to our care.

Later, in Indian summer, at just that time when the sun begins to turn its face away from the world and all of nature begins to speak in a whisper of death and sleep, we teachers begin again, with sharpened No. 2 pencils and a quixotic hope that somehow we will do it better this time. When all of nature is coming to a well needed rest, we are required to practice a Socratic form of midwifery with all the intellectual stretching and pain that the metaphor implies.

In September I will look out at new, eager faces. They will be no older than last year's visages. They will hoodwink me into believing, at least for a while, that I am getting no older. Then one morning before class I will notice, as if for the first time, how the dew is now frozen on the morning lawn. I'll look in the mirror while shaving one morning to realize I could never be confused with Dorian Gray.

By September I will have purposely forgotten how difficult it is in May to give up my good students. By then I will be thinking of ways to make a small difference in the lives of my new students. In the next four years, some will experience the death of parents, others the death of dreams. With that curious divining rod, the mind, they all will find those few ideas that will make their lives make sense. Out of nothing more than protoplasm and those ideas the lucky ones will get to manufacture new dreams.

But most of my new students will travel through their four years with little inkling that their teachers are intimately involved in an almost holy process of grasping and then letting go, of small deaths and tiny resurrections. Most of my students will have no inkling that their teachers have been living in the real world all along.